The Drowned Violin

Mel Malton

Napoleon

Toronto, Ontario, Canada

Cover art: Christopher Chuckry
Cover design: Trudy Agyeman

Published by Napoleon Publishing
Toronto, Ontario, Canada

Le Conseil des Arts | The Canada Council
du Canada | for the arts
depuis 1957 | since 1957

Napoleon Publishing acknowledges the support of the Canada Council for our publishing program

Printed in Canada

10 09 08 07 06   5 4 3 2 1

Library and Archives Canada Cataloguing in Publication

Malton, H. Mel, date-
     The drowned violin / Mel Malton.

(An Alan Nearing mystery)
ISBN 1-894917-23-5

     I. Title. II. Series.

PS8576.A5362D76 2006   jC813'.54   C2006-900038-7

A note to readers

The fictional Town of Laingford is loosely based on Huntsville, Ontario. You won't find Sadler's island or the Weems house, though, no matter how hard you look, because they're made up. All the people in the book are made up, too, like the story is.

However, there is an amazing Pioneer Village in Huntsville, as well as several excellent ice-cream places and a great lookout spot, if you want the perfect view to go with your double-chocolate cone.

Many thanks to Anne Millyard and Christopher Thorpe, for their encouragement. The story was conceived during the first ever Muskoka Novel Marathon, a wildly fun writers' challenge which is now a successful annual fundraising event in support of Muskoka literacy programs. You can find out more about the event at www.huntsvillefestival.on.ca.

And as always, many thanks to my editor, Allister Thompson, and publisher Sylvia McConnell, who didn't bat an eye when I said I was breaking out of the mold and writing a YA novel.

One

A bright green canoe sliced through the waters of Steamboat Lake, the three canoeists paddling hard, as if they were racing. There was no other boat in sight, though.

"Hey, you guys! Stop paddling for a second," said the kid in the stern. He plunged his paddle straight down into the water, putting on the brakes. "There's something weird floating in the water over there, see it?"

Alan and Josée, in bow and centre, quit and turned to look at Ziggy, who was pointing with his paddle.

"Zig, come on! We have to get to the dock before my mom shows up," Alan said. Then he turned back to his work, making a face like a camel to blow a flop of hair out of his eyes, a habit that drove his mother crazy. They were all eleven years old—classmates and summer friends. It was Ziggy's canoe—on permanent loan from his grandfather.

"No wait, I see it," Josée said. "It looks dead, whatever it is." Alan stopped in mid-stroke and turned back to look. Dead? His heart told him that if he wasn't there on the dock at five o'clock, his mom would have a nuclear meltdown, but his brain wasn't listening. Something was floating there, for sure—off to the right, or starboard, as Ziggy would insist on saying. Something too interesting for a detective-type like himself, destined to be a private eye, to ignore.

Ziggy and Josée did something complicated with their paddles to bring the canoe closer. The thing in the water did look dead, as Josée had said, but it wasn't a beaver or a duck. In fact, Alan didn't think it was an animal at all. It looked oddly familiar.

The bow of the canoe came within a paddle's distance, and Alan reached his paddle out to bring the thing in. It was floating just below the surface, with a smooth curve like a belly poking up and catching the late afternoon light, shining in a way that suggested something hard— not fur, but wood, maybe, or plastic. He placed his paddle across the gunwales and stretched his right arm out over the side of the canoe to get hold of it. It wasn't a dead animal, that was for sure, or he would never have put his hand anywhere near it. It looked like a box. A jewellery box, maybe, from some long-ago sunken steamer trunk? Something full of diamonds, or stolen rubies? The wake from the canoe was making the thing bob further away. Alan's imagination went into overdrive, and he stretched just a little more than was smart.

"Hey, watch it, Nearing, you moron. You're tipping us." Almost too late, Alan pulled his hand back and shifted his body back into the centre of the canoe. At the same time, the thing turned over, like a hooked trout does just before it makes a dive for the bottom.

"Holy cow—it's a violin!" Alan shouted. There was no

doubt about it. It was obviously broken—the whole bottom half of the thing was smashed in, but what remained of it was unmistakably violin-shaped—that distinctive curve, the long neck (broken, too) with the curly wooden carving at the end, and the pegs to hold the strings.

"*Sans blague?*" Josée said, doing another sideways paddle-stroke. "Let's move in again, Zig, so Alain can grab it. Just don't lean out so much this time, hey?"

"What's a violin doing in the middle of Steamboat Lake?" Alan said, reaching again.

"How should I know? I'm just the driver," Ziggy said, doing his grandfather-impression. "Okay, grab it now!" Alan tried, and this time his fingers closed around the neck, but the violin gave a slight twitch, as if it were alive, and slipped out of his grasp. And this time, the thing didn't turn over, it simply sank, quickly and decisively, like the *Titanic*.

"Crud," Alan said. "So much for that. We'll never know what that was all about now—it must be about fifty feet deep here."

"Too bad," Josée said. "But you have one of your own already. That one didn't look like it could be fixed."

"Oh, I don't think it was a valuable violin," Alan said. "The pegs were plastic, I think, and it had that look, you know, like the cheap ones have. Still, it was very weird to find it floating out in the middle of the lake."

"Yeah, well, weird or not," Ziggy said, "we'd better get going. You'll be lucky if your Mom doesn't break your neck just like that drowned fiddle."

"Hey, *you* were the one who had to stop…" Alan said.

3

"*Mes amis…*" Josée said. "Don't argue, paddle!" They did.

They were quite a long way out from shore, just coming around a rocky outcrop before preparing to make a straightaway for McGregor beach. From there, it would be a brief paddle up the Kuskawa River to the dock by the boathouse, where Ziggy had permission to keep his canoe for the summer. Without the delay, they could have made it on time. Alan could just hear his mom—"you are such a difficult person," she would say. "I can't rely on you, and that means it's difficult for me to give you any leeway." What she would mean was that he was about to be grounded until he was twenty-seven. Especially if she found out they'd been canoeing out of bounds, out on the lake past the beach.

The green canoe entered the channel at MacGregor Beach at a pretty impressive speed, considering the size of the paddlers.

*   *   *

Alan and Ziggy had been spending their summers in Ziggy's canoe out at Mud Lake since they were nine. This year, for the first time, Ziggy's grandfather had allowed them to keep the canoe in town, by the river. Josée's mother was okay with it (she had said "my daughter was born in a canoe"), so the three of them had been given the go-ahead to paddle down the river as far as McGregor beach, as long as they wore life jackets absolutely *always*.

They had taken a safety course. They had been given

certificates. They were also very determined people, which is why Alan's mom (the only holdout) had eventually said, "Okay, you can paddle your own canoe," which she seemed to think was extremely funny.

On the river, they could go wherever they wanted, no yellow lines to keep to one side of, no pushy mountain bikers or big speeding cars or skateboard bylaw officers. The only thing they had to watch out for on the water was the Weem Team.

Unfortunately, just as they rounded the bend and canoed past a small group of kids on the beach, the Weem Team found them, and they were toast in two minutes.

They had come from nowhere, like they usually did, riding their jet skis in formation like a bunch of bikers in a gang. Dylan Weems was their leader, a big fifteen-year-old. Dylan and his gang of four spent each summer on the water, chasing loons, ducks and kids in canoes. So far, the marine patrol hadn't caught them, but Alan and his friends hoped it would only be a matter of time.

They buzzed across the bow of the canoe, Dylan in the lead, howling like a wolf and creating a circle of heavy waves. Alan, Josée and Ziggy did their best to stay upright, but it was no use. It was like trying to ride out a storm on the ocean, the waves coming at all angles. Over they went, to a chorus of loud "Woo-hoooo" noises from the Weem Team. The kids watching on the shore had stood up to get a better look, pointing and putting their hands up to their mouths as if they were watching a nasty road accident and expected to see blood.

"They're probably hoping we'll drown," Ziggy muttered

through a mouthful of water. This was just like the worst-case-scenario they had been taught to deal with on the canoe safety course, but it was way harder in the middle of the Kuskawa River than it had been on that safe, sandy beach last summer. It was harder, too, with a bunch of people watching and a gang of bullies on jet skis like a swarm of angry hornets, waiting to see if they had stung you hard enough. There was an adult on the beach, too, who started waving his arms and yelling, but the Weem Team just laughed at him and roared away, heading back out to the lake.

Treading water, the kids worked together on one side, rocking the canoe back and forth rapidly so that the water sloshed out of it in waves like soda spilling from a too-full cup. After a moment or two, there was enough water removed for the canoe to be a little bit buoyant again, and Alan and Ziggy vaulted back into it on the count of three —one from each side at the exact same moment so that they didn't tip it again. Then they leaned out on opposite sides to steady the boat as Josée clambered in. They had kept hold of their paddles, thank goodness (because as Ziggy said afterwards, they would have looked like complete morons, trying to paddle to shore with their hands). Also, fortunately, Ziggy, the smart guy, always kept a small bail-bucket (a scooped out Fleecy bottle, with a handle) on a line attached to the rear seat. As soon as they were in, Josée started bailing, and Ziggy and Alan started paddling, heading for shore.

The really unfortunate part of the whole thing was that the closest landing-place was the one at MacGregor beach, where about a dozen people were standing by, gawking. Nobody looked familiar. Summer visitors, most likely—city kids, who probably thought they were bumpkins anyway, little Laingford versions of Red Green.

The canoe reached the shore quickly, and they got out, and together hoisted the boat to waist height, tipped it to get rid of the rest of the water and launched it again. Then an amazing thing happened. The people on the beach applauded—all of them. They clapped and cheered as if Alan, Josée and Ziggy had just won a marathon or something.

"Way to go!" one of them shouted—a red-haired girl about their age in a green bikini.

"Those guys should be arrested," another girl called.

"Woo hoo!" the others sang. This was different from the "Woo hoo" noise the Weem Team had made while they were buzzing the canoe. This was a cheerleader kind of noise—a "Yay for our side" noise. Alan looked up in surprise and saw that Ziggy and Josée were grinning as widely as he was.

"Hey," Ziggy said. "Good work, guys. They like us, eh?"

"That'll cheese off the Weem Team," Alan said.

"*Sans blague.* That redhead is Dylan's sister," Josée said.

"We'd better get going," Alan said. "We still have about two minutes before my mom goes totally postal."

The red-haired girl waved as they paddled away, and Josée waved back.

"Her name's Monica," she said. "She's in my ballet class. She's *sympathique,* even though she's a rich kid with a creepy older brother." They were paddling hard now, going fast enough to create a bow-wave. Around a bend in the river, they could finally see the boathouse dock.

"There's your mom," Ziggy said. "Set your phasers on stun, people, she's ready to blow."

*   *   *

"Alan Michael Nearing, you are such a difficult person," she said, as soon as they got close enough for her to be heard. "I can't rely on you, at all, can I?"

"I'm really sorry, Mom," Alan said at once. Excuses were worth trying, but it was always a good idea to apologize first. Mrs. Mary-Anne Nearing had a thing about manners.

"I should blooming well think so," she said. People sometimes asked Alan how come he didn't have an English accent, like his mother did. "It's because she was born there," he said. "I was born in Laingford, so I sound like this." He could do a pretty good English accent, though, if he tried. He didn't try anything like that now, though.

"We got swamped, Madame Nearing," Josée said. She was the best of the three of them in dealing with parents. Alan thought it was because she always called them *Madame* or *M'sieu.* "A boat went past *trop vite,* and the waves tipped us over."

Mrs. Nearing's attitude changed from annoyance to worry in a split second, but that was a problem, too.

"I just knew it was dangerous letting you three out there on your own in a canoe," she said. "I knew we were taking a big risk—you're too young. You could have drowned. Are you all right?" Alan gave the others a warning look, which meant "no details". No telling her they were being harrassed by Dylan Weems and his thugs, and no telling her that the dunking had been on purpose. If they told the whole story, they'd never be allowed back in the canoe all summer—at least nowhere further than the end of Ziggy's grandfather's dock, out in the wilderness on boring old Mud Lake.

"We're fine, Mom. Really. We did the routine, you know, the bail and scoop thing, and we were back in the boat in about two minutes. Everything's okay, and we were wearing our life jackets the whole time."

Mrs. Nearing's eyes narrowed as she absorbed this information. "Well, if you were back in the boat in two minutes, then it wasn't that which made you late, was it?" Ouch. Too much information, handed over too quickly, without thinking it over first, Alan thought, referring to a handbook he had at home called "How to be an Effective Operative".

"I guess we just lost track of the time," Alan said. "Really, we're sorry." They were out of the boat and up onto the dock. Together, they pulled the canoe up out of the water and carried it into the boathouse, Ziggy locking the door behind him with his own key. Then Alan hugged his mom—sort of an air-hug, as she was dressed in nice clothes, and his T-shirt and shorts were soaking wet. This was the right move, and he saw that she was softening. He decided to press his luck.

"We still have time to change before the train gets here, though, right? And can Ziggy and Josée come to this thing with us? I have to have someone to talk to, you know. Candace will be all over this violin guy."

"She'd better not be," his mom said. "I don't want either of you pestering him. He's a virtuoso, and they're very highly strung."

"Like his Stradivarius violin, eh?" Ziggy said, who had heard all about the famous violinist from Alan. The virtuoso, Hugh Pratt, was coming to town to perform in a concert specially arranged by the Laingford Music Appreciation Society. A local businessman had donated a huge amount of money to hire a whole orchestra and a conductor to come up from the city, Alan had said. Mrs. Nearing, who was the vice-president of the Society, had volunteered to pick Pratt up at the train station and had volunteered her kids to help carry the luggage. They would be expected to attend the welcoming reception, too. Alan knew his sister Candace would be into it, but he wasn't. He liked the Music Society concerts, but their social events were boring—definitely not kid-friendly.

That was why Alan had promised not to be late—not to hold things up so that Hugh Pratt would not be left waiting at the station. He looked at his watch (still ticking after being dunked in the river), and it was only a quarter after five, so they were only fifteen minutes later than he'd said they would be.

"When's the train, Mom? We do have time still, right?"

Mrs. Nearing grinned suddenly, a sly glint in her eye. "The train's not till six," she said. "I knew you'd be late, my lad, no matter what kind of threats I threw at you. So you three have exactly half an hour to dry off and put on something decent before we have to leave. Yes, Ziggy and

Josée can come, if you have something clean in that disgusting room of yours that will fit them."

"Sweet!" Alan said.

"Indeed. You'll be sweeter after a shower, I think. You smell like gasoline, all of you."

"It's that pure, clean Kuskawa water, Mrs. Nearing," Ziggy said, grinning. "With a little jet ski fuel mixed in."

"Don't get me started on the environmental stuff, Ziggy," she said. "I can't afford to let my blood pressure rise right now. I need to be all calm and pleasant and civilized for the Society's reception."

"Where's the party being held this year, Mom?" Alan asked. "It was at the Mooseview last year," he added in an aside to the others. "The food was amazing."

"Oh, you'll like it, I promise you, love," she said. "It's at Giles Weems's place—that enormous mansion on the lake. I believe he has a teenaged son, Dylan. Do you know him? And I know they've got a pool table down in the basement. You'll find plenty to do."

Two

"I can't believe I'm actually going to meet Hugh Pratt," said Alan's fifteen-year-old sister, Candace. She was sitting in the passenger seat of the van, talking excitedly to her mother and completely ignoring the others in the back.

"It is rather exciting, isn't it, darling?" Mrs. Nearing said. "But don't crowd him, all right? Some musicians are terribly sensitive, you know."

"He better not be too sensitive," Alan muttered. "Your perfume would knock out an army. Did you *take a bath* in that stuff?"

"Alan, you are such a pig," Candace said. But it was true. Candace had kind of overdone it in terms of personal hygiene. Whatever perfume she was wearing had filled the van with its sweet, flowery-candy scent, and Mrs. Nearing had powered down the windows almost as soon as they had backed out of the driveway, although she hadn't mentioned the reason. Alan exchanged a grimace with Ziggy and Josée and made choking sounds.

"Mom! Make him stop," Candace said.

"Oh, I *ask* you. You'd think you were still six years old, all of you," Mrs. Nearing said. "Alan, try to act civilized, at least when we have Mr. Pratt in the car."

Candace had the famous musician's latest CD with her and gazed dreamily at his picture on the front cover.

"I'm going to get him to sign this," she said.

"Well, wait for the right moment," Mrs. Nearing said. "Don't shove the thing at him as soon as he gets off the train."

"Mom. Of course, I wouldn't do that. Give me some credit."

He was good-looking—at least his picture was, Alan thought, staring over at the movie-star profile of the Canadian virtuoso plastered across the front of the CD, all white teeth and gleaming black hair. The musician was wearing a tuxedo, and his famous Stradivarius was under his chin, as if he was in the middle of playing something. Alan knew that it was posed, because you couldn't possibly look that good while you were playing. He had once practiced in front of the mirror, just before a recital, and saw that whenever he played the hard parts, he stuck out his tongue, like he had just burned it. Still, maybe virtuoso violinists learned how to smile and play at the same time. Alan knew he would never be a virtuoso—in fact, he would have given anything to quit violin lessons completely, although he hadn't had the guts to mention this idea to his mother. It was Candace who had the potential, not him. She was already playing solos in the concerts given by their music teacher, Mr. Ziegler, and she took special classes at the Royal Conservatory in the city. Candace had a chance at a first-chair orchestra position, her mother said. Alan, on the other hand, had a chance at maybe being the guy who swept the floor after the show. Still, he kept taking lessons, because he knew his mother would call him "a difficult person" if he told her he wanted to quit.

"So how did this guy get hold of a Stradivarius? Is he, like, a millionaire?" asked Ziggy.

"He won a Canada Council contest," Candace said. "Some American magnate donated the Strad, and they had a big competition for all the young up-and-coming violinists in the country. Hugh Pratt won, and he gets to play the instrument for five years, to help build his career."

"Oh, I get it. So it's a loaner—he doesn't actually own it."

"No, but that's the point, right? When you're young and starting out, there's no way you could afford something like a Strad, but the chance to play an instrument like that for five whole years—can you imagine? I would kill for that kind of opportunity."

"Try not to exaggerate, dear," Mrs. Nearing said. "It's unbecoming."

"Well, I would do anything to get a chance to play a Strad, anyway," she said.

"And what's so special about a Stradivarius?" Ziggy asked. "Apart from the famous name?"

"Nobody really knows," Candace said. "It's like the big mystery of the musical world. Scientists have done all kinds of tests and stuff on the instruments, and they think it has something to do with the varnish the violin-maker used. They were built back in the 1600s, and it's amazing that they still sound so good. People say it's the best string sound in the world—Stradivarius violins, violas, cellos—there's nothing that compares to it. And of course, they're worth bazillions of dollars, so only a very few really famous musicians can afford their own."

"Is that why you're all dressed up like that?" Alan said. Candace, who usually didn't pay too much attention to her looks, was wearing a very short skirt and a crop top that exposed her stomach. She was wearing shoes with big heels, too, and makeup that made her look way older than fifteen. This was not her usual style. "Are you hoping that Hugh Pratt will let you take his instrument for a little spin?"

His mother snorted loudly, then immediately blasted him to kingdom come. He sat quiet for the rest of the journey, folding his arms and frowning, ignoring Ziggy and Josée, who didn't say anything after that, either.

*   *   *

The train was on time, and so were they, so they didn't have to wait around much. Alan and his friends had wanted to stay in the van and let his Mom and Candace do the welcoming. But Mrs. Nearing insisted that they all come.

"He may have a great deal of luggage," she said, "and I want you on hand to help carry it. The days of the railroad porter are long gone, you know, so you'll have to help out."

When the train pulled into the station, they were waiting on the platform in a row, like those plastic ducks some people liked to put on their front lawns—the mother duck and four babies in descending size, although

Ziggy and Josée were not technically Mrs. Nearing's ducklings.

Candace gave a little squeak when she saw Hugh Pratt descend from the train like a royal prince. He was wearing a black leather jacket, baggy black trousers and shiny dark shoes. His hair was mussed in the kind of way that you just know takes a lot of careful planning, and he had a slightly stubbled chin, as if he had forgotten to shave that morning. He had a square, chiselled jaw and large, dark eyes.

"He looks like a model," Josée said to the others.

"Oh wow, he is even more amazing in person than he is in his pictures," Candace said. Her voice had gone all breathy. Alan risked a look at her, although he was determined not to make any more mean comments. He had seen this happen before, when his sister had said she was in love with Leonardo di Caprio. Alan was sure that his remarks then had helped get her over it. Now she was doing the same thing again over this musician, and it would be hard not to bug her about it.

A rail attendant handed down two large suitcases out of the passenger car onto the platform, and Mr. Pratt himself carried a black leather briefcase on a strap over his shoulder, and in his left hand, his violin case.

"Welcome to Laingford, Mr. Pratt," said Mrs. Nearing, and held out her hand.

"Thank God that's over," he said, touching her hand briefly like a guy on the winning team in a post-game handshake. Alan felt a stab of dislike as he saw his mother's welcoming smile get brittle, suddenly, like glass. "The train journey was a total drag, and I was stuck next

16

to this incredibly boring old woman who talked the whole way about her stupid grandchildren." His voice was a slow, drawled-out whine, like a long bow on an untuned string.

"He doesn't sound near as classy as he looks," Ziggy muttered. Alan and Josée nodded in agreement.

"You're the reception party, I take it?" Mr. Pratt went on. "I was expecting a limo. Can you smaller kids handle these bags? They're kind of heavy." Alan and his friends picked up the cases without comment. They *were* heavy, but after a remark like that, they weren't going to let it show. Then the musician turned to Candace, who immediately turned bright red. Alan thought she might be holding her breath. "And if you wouldn't mind taking this, sweetheart, that would be great," he said. Her face was practically glowing, a huge smile plastered on so wide, it looked like it would crack her face in half. The musician was going to let her carry the famous violin for him.

"I knew it," Alan said quietly to the others.

Candace stretched out her arms to receive the precious case, her fingers just touching the corner of it, when Mr. Pratt snatched it away with a look of horror on his face. "Not that," he snapped. "God, I wouldn't let a kid carry the Stradder. No, I meant *this,*" and he handed her his leather briefcase. She looked like she'd been slapped.

"Ouch," Ziggy muttered.

In the van, Mr. Pratt sat in the front with Mrs. Nearing, drawling a long list of complaints about his train journey—from the lousy food in the dining car to the hardness of the seats. Alan reached over and gave his sister a sympathetic punch on the shoulder. It was just a tap—no big deal, and luckily she knew exactly what he meant and gave him a twisted and slightly misty-eyed smile. That should make up for the remark he'd made earlier, he thought. Sisters. Unpredictable people.

In the back seat, they all kept a kind of stony silence, while Mr. Pratt talked on and on. Alan's mother didn't seem to have noticed that anything was wrong with Candace, and she seemed to have forgotten Mr. Pratt's snobby handshake. She was chatting quite pleasantly to him, asking him about the upcoming concert, and whether he was looking forward to working with the Society orchestra. Maybe mothers don't notice the same things kids do, Alan thought. She didn't seem to have any problem with this man at all.

*   *   *

When they got to the Weems' place, which was a huge glass and wood home on the shores of Steamboat Lake, Mr. Pratt seemed to get bigger, somehow. His voice changed, and he started purring, like a large, sleek cat.

"This is my kind of place," he said.

"Yes, it's lovely, isn't it?" Mrs. Nearing said, in a friendly voice. "I'm sure you'll be very comfortable here, Mr. Pratt. They have a beautiful guest room." A couple of women, standing in the driveway, pointed at the Nearing's vehicle and waved to Mrs. Nearing. "Got him, then?" one of the women called out.

"Safe and sound," Mrs. Nearing called back. "Come

on over and meet him before anybody else does." The women began to stroll over in their direction. Alan watched as Mr. Pratt, who was still doing his contented cat imitation, checked out his reflection in the side view mirror before getting out of the van.

Candace, who had been sitting behind the drivers' seat, the furthest from the door, got out last, after the boys. Somehow, she got her foot wrapped around one of the seat belts, which was dragging on the floor, and she fell sideways suddenly, missed her footing and landed in a heap on the asphalt driveway, crying out in pain as she landed. Mr. Pratt moved right in on her.

"Oh, angel, are you all right?" he said, all the whine gone from his voice and replaced by a honey-sweet tone that seemed to make Candace forget her pain.

"I—my foot," she said. He crouched down next to her, all concern and hands. Mrs. Nearing had missed the fall, having walked over to meet the advancing women, and all three arrived back at the van just as Pratt was helping Candace to her feet.

"What on earth happened, Candace?" Mrs. Nearing said. "Have you hurt yourself?"

"I tripped on something in the van and fell and twisted my foot or ankle or something," Candace said, "but Mr. Pratt helped me. I'm fine." And truly, she looked better than she had in a while, Alan thought. She had her Leonardo di Caprio smile on again.

"Call me Hugh, please," Mr. Pratt said to her, all the time seeming to keep half an eye on the ladies who had come over, as if he wanted them to see how nice he was being. Is it only me who is noticing this stuff? Alan thought. He felt like a superhero all of a sudden, with special powers that nobody else had. Great. Other guys get bitten by a radioactive spiders and end up being able to climb buildings. Alan Nearing gets buzzed by a bunch of bullies on jet skis, and all he ends up with is a hyperactive sensitive-o-meter.

"Thanks, Hugh," Candace said. "I think I can walk on it if I go really slowly." She leaned on his arm and began walking with him towards the door, surrounded by Mrs. Nearing and the other women. Mr. Pratt had left his briefcase and the violin case on the ground beside Alan and his friends. They unloaded the rest of the bags from the back of the van and prepared to carry it all in.

"Excuse me, Mr. Pratt," Alan called out to the musician, who had his arm wrapped around his sister's waist. The musician turned his head and raised an eyebrow at him.

"Yes, er, Al?" All four of them had been introduced to him at the train station. Alan hated "Al", but this wasn't the time to say so.

"What about your 'Stradder'? You want to carry it yourself, or is it okay for one of us kids to bring it in?"

Mrs. Nearing frowned at Alan and gave her head a little shake, but Mr. Pratt just smiled.

"Er, that will be fine, buddy," he said. "Just be very, very careful with it, okay? And bring it straight on in, okay?"

Alan picked up the violin case carefully, like it might explode, and cradled it in his arms. "As if I was going to run away with it or something," he said to Ziggy and Josée. "It's not me that has a crush on his stupid violin, it's Candace. And Mr. Pratt looks like he's suddenly got a crush on her."

"Maybe he'll let her play it, then," Josée said.

"Yeah, and then she breaks it and has to go to jail. I can see it now. I'd be the brother of a criminal."

"That would be good for a detective, wouldn't it?" Ziggy said. "You'd be able to visit her in jail and get to know the real bad guys—how they work, and stuff."

"You'd only get to meet the bad *girls,*" Josée said. "She'd be in a youth detention centre, not like where mamère works." Josée's mother had just started a kitchen job at the men's prison down the highway in Wenonah.

"Too bad," said Alan. "I'd really like to find a way to visit that place. It would be cool to see what happens to the bad guys I'll be tracking down some day."

"You'll be visiting them full-time if you don't watch where you're going with that violin," said Mrs. Nearing, coming up behind them.

Three

A lan and Ziggy and Josée put the luggage down by the door. The virtuoso had deposited Candace on a bench in the entranceway and was swallowed up by a group of adults, who were all shaking his hand. Alan carried the violin case over and handed it directly to Mr. Pratt, who took it with a nod.

"Go on in," Mrs. Nearing said, and they slipped past the crowd and into a big hallway.

Candace stayed on the bench in a dreamy haze, although Alan privately thought that she was mostly faking the foot thing.

The hallway opened onto a huge living room, crammed with people. There was a floor-to-ceiling stone fireplace and a wall of windows, leading out to a stone patio big enough for a hockey game.

An enormous gas barbecue stood in one corner, by a railing overlooking the lake. To Alan, it looked like a backyard cookout in a movie: too glossy to be real. Everything seemed to be three times its normal size, from the barbecue itself, which was bigger than the whole kitchen counter at home, to the tall stacks of steaks, shrimp, burgers, sausages and vegetable kebabs waiting to be cooked on the grill. No matter how boring the evening might turn out to be, at least the food would be good. Alan's mouth started watering.

"I'm starving," he said.

"Me, too," Ziggy said. They started weaving through the crowd, making for the barbecue.

"What if we meet up with Dylan Weems?" Josée said.

"You won't—he's down at the boathouse," came a girl's voice from beside them. They turned, and there was Monica Weems, the girl with the red hair from the beach. "My mother said there would be kids my age coming. Hi, Josée."

"Ça va, Monique?" she said. They both slipped into French, and Alan and Ziggy were lost for a sentence or two.

"Sorry, guys," Josée said after a moment. "Monica's in French immersion at her school in Toronto, so we do this sometimes."

"Makes me feel like a moron," Ziggy complained.

"It's not my fault you hate Madame Simard," she shot back. At their own school, Josée was the French teacher's pet, according to Ziggy.

"You guys hungry?" Monica said. Good move, Alan thought. Josée and Ziggy were no fun when they got on to that subject.

There was a bar with a friendly bartender, who offered them four kinds of pop, and there was a whole banquet table crowded with salads, breads and desserts. A man in a chef's hat was in charge of the grill, waving a spatula in the air and occasionally splashing stuff from a bottle onto the cooking meat, which made fragrant flames shoot up into the evening air.

Soon, they all had plates of food. "Let's go out on the lawn—there's a place we can eat where there won't be so many people," Monica said.

But before they managed to make their way to the end of the patio, someone clinked a glass with a fork to get everybody's attention, and the crowd went quiet.

Mr. Pratt made his entrance.

"He's changed his clothes already," Josée whispered. "*Quel* show-off."

"How come you notice these things?" Alan whispered back.

"I'm just observant, that's all—the way you should be, if you're planning to open your own detective agency."

"I'm observant. I just find it hard to look at him. He's creepy."

"I've met him before," Monica whispered. "You're right. Who's that girl with him?"

"My sister," Alan said. An adult in front of them turned around and shushed them.

The man who had tinked the glass made a long speech. Alan knew the man must be Monica's father, Mr. Weems, because she kept making little huffy, embarrassed noises, the longer he went on. Finally he finished, and everybody clapped and started talking again.

"I hate it when he does that," Monica said. "Come on." They followed her out onto the lawn to a secluded picnic table by the side of the house.

"This is a staff area, but I like it because it's quiet," she said.

Monica told them about her school in the city—the one her mother had attended.

"I don't know many people up here," she said. "That's why I take summer ballet. I'm supposed to make friends." She said it sadly, as if she hadn't found any.

"You can come with us when we do stuff, if you want," Josée said. Alan and Ziggy exchanged dark looks. Monica seemed okay, but four in the canoe would be crowded, and Josée acted more, well, like a girl when there was another girl around. It wasn't as if Alan and Ziggy were interested in ballet. Alan's violin lessons were bad enough.

"If I'm allowed," Monica said, "that would be great." Alan figured she probably wasn't allowed to hang around with local kids, anyway. Except for ballet dancers.

"Who were you at the beach with, then?" he asked. Monica looked surprised.

"Oh, I was sort of babysitting—our gardener's little girl. It was her day off, so my mother volunteered me to go along and look after Taylor. I think mother just wanted me out of the house."

"Aren't you a bit young for babysitting?" Ziggy said.

"I'm twelve," Monica said. "Mother says I act like I'm twenty, though." There was no answer to that, and anyway, she *did* seem a lot older than they were. Maybe it was because she was dressed up like Candace was.

"You said you'd met the violinist before," Alan said. "Have you heard him play?"

"No—I'm not really into classical music," Monica said. "My father plays opera CDs full blast Saturday mornings and it drives me crazy."

"Ouch," Ziggy said.

"Do *you* like that kind of music?" Monica asked Alan.

"He plays," Ziggy said.

"I'm lousy at it, though," Alan said at once. "But I like it if the person playing knows what he's doing. Or she. My sister's pretty good."

"She's amazing," Josée said. "She'll probably be famous like Mr. Pratt, one day."

"Is that why she was following him around like a puppy dog up there?" Monica said. Yep, Alan thought. Monica Weems acts a lot older than she looks. A lot snobbier, too.

A woman in a glittery dress called to them from the balcony and beckoned to Monica.

"Shoot," she said. "Mother wants me. You can go get more food if you want. I'll probably be awhile. Maybe later you can come down to the boathouse with me. See ya." She left her paper plate on the table and made her way back up to the patio.

"She's weird," Ziggy said.

"She's lonely, that's all," Josée said.

*   *   *

They went back for seconds and watched as the guest of honour strolled around, being introduced to people, shaking hands. Every so often he would throw back his head, toss his floppy black hair and laugh at something someone had said. When he did so, every head would turn. He had a weird laugh, slightly metallic, as if the

26

laughter was being piped in through a really tinny pair of speakers.

"Monica was right, Alain," Josée said, suddenly. A kind of shadow was following the musician around—well not a shadow really, because she was perfectly solid. Candace. She was carrying that black leather briefcase thing, and they saw her bring him a pen when he asked for one, beckoning to her like she was a servant.

"What is *with* her?" Alan said. "She's acting like his maid. Is she nuts?"

"A brush with fame will bring you shame," Ziggy said, in his grandfather voice. "Look, I bet now she's being asked to do something else." Mr. Pratt had taken the pen (to autograph a CD), then muttered something quietly to Candace, leaning down to whisper in her ear. Candace became even more radiant as he did so—sort of eager, Alan thought. Like she's picturing herself as a rising star and Mr. Pratt as the famous coach. She started moving in their direction, although she didn't notice them as she passed. With a determined look in her eyes, Candace headed for the bar, the leather briefcase slung like a big purse over her shoulder.

"A glass of white wine for Mr. Pratt, please," she said with confidence. There were two men standing at the bar table, who looked like they were waiting to be served, and she butted right in front of them.

"There's no way she looks old enough. Even with the makeup," Josée said.

The bartender picked up one of the open bottles sitting in the ice barrel and poured some wine into a long-stemmed glass. He handed it to Candace without a word and took the next drink order from the man standing behind her. She obviously wasn't interested in drinking it herself—anyone could see that just by looking at her, Alan thought. She looked like she was carrying something holy. First it was his briefcase. Then his wine glass. What was next? His violin, probably. Which she'd break, then go to jail.

Carrying the Stradivarius violin case in from the van had not been such a big deal. It wasn't heavy, and he hadn't felt any strange alien vibrations from the instrument nestled inside. Still, he had to admit he'd felt relieved when he had handed it over to Mr. Pratt in the hallway.

"Hey, we could try what your sister just pulled off, eh?" Ziggy said. "Just go up and ask for a glass of wine for Mr. Pratt."

"I doubt it would work," Alan said. "Anyway, who wants to drink wine? Yuck."

"I've tried it," Josée said. "It's sour and awful."

"I just like doing stuff I'm not supposed to do," Ziggy said.

"Well, not here, okay?" Alan said. "Mom would kill us."

"And you'd puke," Josée added.

"So what do we do if Dylan shows up?" Ziggy said when they had refilled their plates. Josée and Alan had slices of chocolate cake, and Ziggy had another pile of shrimp, as well as cake. Alan thought his friend might be sick anyway, even if he didn't get to try a glass of wine. They stayed up on the patio to eat. The picnic table had felt too private, not a good place to be if Dylan found them.

"Monica said he was in the boathouse," Josée said.

"Yeah, and she wants to take us down there," Alan said. "Why?"

"Maybe she wants to lure us into the Weem Team's torture chamber," Ziggy said.

"Ew. *Quel* thought."

"There she is," Alan said a few minutes later, pointing. Monica was threading through the crowd, heading straight for Mr. Pratt, who was signing autographs again. Candace was standing at his side like an honour guard. They were standing under a tree at the furthest corner of the patio, just in front of a set of stairs leading down to the waterfront. At the bottom of the stairs was a complicated series of docks, several boats and the boathouse, which was bigger than many of the houses on Alan's street. The tree was a huge maple, with its branches reaching out over the party-goers, tiny white lights twisted in the branches. A sunset was beginning to develop like a photograph over the lake—it was still light out, but it was that kind of golden light that reminded Alan of warm maple syrup.

When Monica walked up and touched Mr. Pratt's arm to get his attention, Alan thought he saw his sister stiffen slightly, like Picasso the family cat did when a neighbouring cat invaded his territory.

"What's she saying, do you think?" Ziggy said.

The violinist bent his head to hear Monica's message, putting his arm around her shoulders as he did so. Monica leaned away, not looking very happy.

"Hmm," Josée said. "He is creepy. Touchy-creepy."

Mr. Pratt put his other arm around Candace, who looked a bit unsteady. Alan wondered if her hurt foot was real, after all. The three of them seemed to be having an intense conversation.

"You know, this would be good practice," Ziggy said.

"For what?"

"For when you're a detective and you have to keep someone under observation. We should sneak up real close from the other side of the tree without them seeing us, and try to hear what they're saying."

"That would be eavesdropping," Josée said.

"Not for the detective, it wouldn't be," Ziggy countered. "We'll be his assistants. Information gathering, eh?"

"And if they catch us spying on them?"

"We just pretend it was a coincidence. Come on. It'll be fun." They wouldn't really have to do much skulking around, just make their way around the edge of the crowd to where the tree was, then stand behind it. They'd be able to hear everything Mr. Pratt and the girls said.

There were a few people wandering around on the lawn, admiring the flower beds and strolling down the grassy slope, or taking the stairs to look at the boats. Alan began to make his way towards the tree, weaving his way past the chattering groups of adults. Maybe he didn't have to sneak around at all—real detectives didn't hide what they were doing, at least not the ones in his favourite books. The P.I. types in books just walked up to a suspect and asked them all sorts of nosy questions. And the people usually answered them, too. But that was when there was a crime under investigation. The only crime here was that Mr. Pratt was being creepy, and probably none of the adults noticed.

"Hey, I thought we were sneaking up on them," Ziggy said, as Alan changed course.

"I thought it would be easier to go up and say hi, instead of sneaking around," Alan said. But there was no point in doing either by then, because the next time they got a clear view of the spot under the tree, Hugh Pratt was talking to a husband-and-wife couple in matching shirts, and both girls had disappeared.

Four

A lan felt a tap on his shoulder. He turned around, and it was Monica.

"I thought you'd like to know, Mr. Pratt is playing for the guests out on the patio in a little while, if you want to stay and hear it. We can go down to the boathouse later, okay?" She smiled and slipped away.

"Great. She snuck up on us," Ziggy said. "She wouldn't even have seen us if we'd been doing it the right way."

"That was nice of her," Josée said. "I wouldn't mind hearing what a million dollars sounds like."

"I doubt you could tell the Stradder is worth a million bucks, just by hearing it," Ziggy said.

"Can you imagine—all that money for a musical instrument?" Josée said. "When there are children starving in the Third World?"

"Do you think these people care about that?" Ziggy said. "How could you live in a house like this and at the same time be worried about starving Third World people?"

"Monica cares," Josée said. "She's really into that stuff. She joined the Peace Child International website and everything. You should ask her about it, Zig."

"It must be hard to be rich if you feel like that, eh?" he said. "Does she send them her allowance or something?"

"Ask her—here she comes."

"Let's go and grab a bench before they all get taken," Monica said, grabbing Josée's arm and dragging her up the stairs onto the patio. Alan and Ziggy followed. Monica looked at Alan. "He asked your sister to go get the violin from his room. Is she like his personal assistant or something?"

"She seems to think so," Alan said.

"Sucks being her," Monica said. Alan wasn't allowed to use that word, and neither were the others. "Anyway," Monica went on, "he's going to play a caterpillar or something."

"A capella, probably," Alan said. "It means unaccompanied. By himself."

"You sound just like your violin teacher," Ziggy said, laughing.

*"A capella...*that sounds like what he said. I always feel stupid at these things, but Mother always wants me to 'mingle'. She says it's a social skill I'm supposed to learn, but I'm not very good at it."

"Hey, you can mingle with us any time," Josée said.

"Yeah. We'll be the four minglers," Ziggy said. *Traitor,* Alan thought.

"Regarde, Alain. Not every female in the world is a big fan of Mr. Pratt, I see," Josée said.

Mr. Pratt was having some sort of confrontation with a very angry young woman with short blonde hair and glasses, who was standing very close to him.

33

"What do you think, *Monsieur le détective?* Lovers' tiff?"

"I think she's one of the members of the orchestra," Alan said. "I helped do the set-up stuff when the orchestra members came up to Laingford a couple of days ago, for the rehearsal. And I remember meeting her. She's the first chair violin. She's really good." And she—her name was Annette something—had also been really nice to Alan, treating him like someone whose opinion mattered. He had been setting up the strings of little clip-on lights that were attached to the orchestra music stands, so that they would be able to read the music when the stage lights were dim. She had come onstage early, had her case open and was cursing quietly to herself, and he'd looked up to see if he had done something wrong.

"Oh, it's not you," she'd said, when she saw his stricken face. "I just forgot to loosen one of my bows yesterday. Really stupid. Now the hairs are stretched, and it's toast. I'll have to get it restrung."

"Oh, I do that all the time," Alan had said, without thinking.

"You play, do you?" They had chatted about music and instruments, and Alan had given her the name of the violin guy who did repairs for the music shop in Laingford.

"Well, whoever she is, she's really mad, I think," Josée said.

Annette wasn't shouting at Mr. Pratt, exactly, but people were looking.

She suddenly seemed to realize they were being watched, laughed a little recklessly and turned to go, almost knocking over Candace, who had returned carrying the Stradivarius

34

case. Mr. Pratt leaped forward to save the instrument, which had started to fall to the ground, throwing his arms around the instrument and Candace herself.

Annette spun around to face him again, with a snarl on her face that Alan, even some distance away, thought was frightening.

"Flirting with the girls again, Hugh? Haven't you learned yet?" This time her voice was loud enough to make sure everybody heard. Conversations stopped. "But oh, yes, I forgot," she went on, still at full volume, "that's how you won the competition in the first place, isn't it? Too bad you didn't win based on your talent." With that she turned once more and made a fast exit, almost tripping on the steps by the patio doors. A man wearing a black leather jacket—Alan thought he was one of the other orchestra players—stepped out of one of the silent, watching groups and followed her.

"Wow," said Ziggy. "That was better than *Masterpiece Theatre.* Flirting with the girls, eh? I bet Candace doesn't mind."

"My mom would," Alan said, looking around to see if he could spot her in the crowd.

Monica made a choked, laughing sound.

Mr. Pratt watched Annette retreat up the steps, shook his head sadly, then touched Candace's shoulder.

"An old flame," he said, loudly enough for everybody watching to hear. "And she's probably had too much to drink. She's a little on the flaky side at the best of times. Sorry about that. You're okay, eh?" Candace just nodded and gave him a radiant smile.

Alan remembered the way he had felt when they came into the house, like he was in the middle of a movie set, everything too big and shiny. He felt like that again, now. The whole day had been so—dramatic. Starting from the moment that he and Ziggy and Josée had found the broken, drowned violin in the water, then Dylan Weems and his friends swamping the canoe, then meeting Mr. Pratt at the train station, and all the stuff about the stupid Stradder violin, and now this scene like a soap opera right in front of them. He felt tired, suddenly.

Still, there was a plus side. He was with his friends, he was anything but bored, and Hugh Pratt, virtuoso violinist, was about to give everybody a free concert. He may not be a great violin student, but he did like to hear good playing—it made shivers run up and down his spine. He didn't want to be a concert violinist himself, but hearing one made him feel like he was part of a special kind of club.

Mr. Pratt had tuned the violin quietly in a corner of the patio, and stood now with head bowed, holding the Stradder at his side. Mr. Weems got up to speak again. He was a very large man, with steel grey, crew-cut hair and one of those necks that seemed to be as wide as his head.

He introduced Mr. Pratt all over again, even though he had already done it when the musician had first arrived. "Father loves to speak in public," Monica muttered. "I wish he wouldn't. He never knows when to stop."

"It is Sylvia's and my very great privilege to be able to provide accommodation to Mr. Pratt during his stay in Laingford," Mr. Weems said. "And we are proud to be able to say that we believe we are the first people in Kuskawa to house, under their very own roof, a priceless instrument built in Italy over three hundred and twenty years ago. Mr. Pratt has very kindly consented to let us hear its voice, through his own magnificent talent, as a little preview to Friday's concert."

The sunset was at its peak, a symphony of crazy colours, purple, pink and orange reflecting off the still lake like a postcard picture you'd never believe was real. The air was warm, and the scent of clean water and pine needles drifted in from the shore, mixing with the smell of spicy food, women's perfume and cigars. For once, the lake was silent, no jet skis or late night powerboats. Alan wondered if this peacefulness had something to do with the fact that the Weem Team was (according to Monica) holed up in the boathouse instead of tearing up and down the lake.

After Mr. Weems's introduction, there was a bit more applause, then silence descended. Mr. Pratt had been waiting for what seemed like minutes, but was probably only a few seconds, for some inner timer to go off, maybe. The Stradivarius was held lightly in his left hand, his hand delicately cradling the neck, the bow in his right. It was so quiet that Alan could hear the wind brushing through the needles of a white pine on the hill, a sad, haunting sound, very high up, and sort of lost. Out on the lake, a loon began to call, its wild, lonely cry making the hairs on the back of Alan's neck stand up by themselves. That was Pratt's cue, maybe the one he had unconsciously been waiting for. He lifted the violin so that it rested underneath his chin. He brought the bow very gently to the strings, closed his eyes and began to play.

*   *   *

What had Candace said about the Stradivarius violin? The best string sound in the world? Alan had heard a lot of violin music in his eleven years. His mother was always playing violin CDs at home, had done so ever since he could remember. He knew the difference between Bach, Handel, Brahms and Beethoven, the voice of the violin as much a part of who he was as whatever DNA-stuff his parents had passed on to him. Candace had been given her first baby violin, a tiny instrument like a toy, when she was four, before Alan was born. She'd taken to it right away, Mrs. Nearing often boasted, playing nursery songs and jingles she heard on the TV. As soon as he was a toddler, Alan had wanted to do what his big sister was doing, so the baby violin had come to him when Candace moved up to a larger instrument.

Candace had taught him to play "Twinkle, Twinkle, Little Star", and then he had started taking lessons from Mr. Ziegler up on Lookout Hill. He had never been violin-crazy, like his sister, but he'd enjoyed it until just recently, when it had suddenly started becoming a chore.

The first note from Hugh Pratt's Stradivarius was almost too quiet to hear: the very softest, lowest note on the scale, an answer to the loon out on the lake. Then it swelled, filling the night air with a sound that Alan felt you could almost touch, if you put out your hand to feel

38

it. The note broke into a series of trills and ripples, like water, and the musician was off into a complicated piece of music, unfamiliar and haunting—not Bach or Beethoven, something wilder.

Mr. Pratt's playing transformed him. Gone was the person who had emerged from the train, demanding a limo. Gone was the man who had been rude to Alan's mom and bossed his sister around. Instead, here a musician who could made a violin sound like a human voice. Hearing it, Alan began to understand what people meant when they talked of the Strad being something special—something apart from the ordinary. Of course, Mr. Pratt's talent was half of it, but Alan had never heard such a sound coming from a stringed instrument, not even in the best recordings. It gave him goose bumps. The music lifted up and carried out over the water like a beam of light. It was bright and brilliant and sad and melancholy, all at once, and in the middle of it, at one point when the bow stilled for a moment, resting on the strings as if an invisible hand had stopped it, the loon called again. The Strad answered. And again, and the wild bird and the priceless violin seemed to play a duet together. Then the last note died away, and the music was finished.

During the applause, Monica tugged at Alan's elbow.

"Hey, you guys, follow me down to the boathouse. It'll be way more interesting down there—trust me."

"Isn't your brother down there?" Ziggy asked.

"Not now," she said. "They're playing pool in the basement. This is the only chance we'll get. There's something I want to show you."

All the people who had been strolling on the grounds were now on the patio, and the crowd was pretty thick. They wormed their way through it and out onto the grass.

"Hurry," Monica said, "before my brother and his friends get back. They'll kill us if they catch us."

"More drama," Ziggy said, and shook his head like an old man. Alan nodded glumly, and they followed Monica and Josée down to the lake.

Five

Behind them, the party continued, with the chatter of conversation, the occasional clinking of bottles and glasses and some soft classical music—recorded, not live. Mr. Pratt's tinny laughter could be heard rising above the party noise.

Ahead of them, the boathouse loomed at the shore like a huge bullfrog waiting for flies. The sun was all the way down now in a navy-blue-black sky, and the two boathouse windows, lit from inside, looked like glowing eyes.

Monica was leading, Josée next. "You're sure your brother isn't down here, right?" Ziggy called from behind Alan. Monica stopped and waited for the boys to catch up.

"Yes, I'm sure. I've been watching the boathouse all this time, waiting for them to leave. You'll see why in a minute. Dylan's playing pool in the rec room with his friends now. I saw them. They'll be down there for hours."

"What was it you wanted to show us?" Josée said.

"Come in here, and you'll see," she said.

They went through a side door and found themselves in a watery, echoey place with high ceilings, lit with floor lights so it felt like a stage. Two big boats floated heavily in their moorings, gleaming and splooshing like they were alive, and at the end, several jet skis bobbed.

"They look like mean ducks," Josée said, pointing. On the deck was a pile of lifejackets, paddles, three kayaks and a couple of canoes.

"You could have a regatta right here," Ziggy said.

"It's upstairs," Monica said, leading them to a staircase. Over the boats, on the second floor, was a small apartment—a living area, with a few doors leading off to the back, and a small kitchen. A big window looked out over the lake.

"Wow," Josée said. "You could live here, Monica."

"It's guest quarters, but nobody uses it much except Dylan. Dad sometimes sleeps down here if he's going fishing in the morning, but it's mostly Dylan's."

"Sweet," Ziggy said.

"And he lets you come up here?" Alan said.

"I'm allowed to, although Dylan hates it when I do," she said. "And I don't, when he's around. His friends are pretty scary."

"So what are we doing here?" Ziggy said, looking around as if one of Dylan's friends might be lying in wait for them.

"I found this yesterday, and I don't know if I should tell," she said. She led them into a small bedroom off the main living area. The room was very dim, but she didn't turn on the light until she had closed the blinds. Then she opened the closet.

It was full of televisions and CD players, power tools and boxes of what looked like bottles.

"So? It's a load of stuff," Ziggy said.

"Yes, but what's it doing here?" Monica said. "It's not Dad's. There's a TV in every room in the house, practically, and Dad doesn't touch power tools."

"It's Dylan's, right?" Josée said after a moment. "Why would he want to buy all this?"

"That's why I wanted to show it to you. I don't think he bought it."

"He stole it?" Alan said. A real crime. His first real case. He felt his chest tighten with excitement.

"There have been a lot of cottage break-ins this summer. I heard Mother and Dad talking about it the other night. It was on the news, and Dad is organizing a neighbourhood watch group on the lake."

"But if it's Dylan doing the break-ins, then…" Alan began.

"…then Dad doesn't have to worry about his own property getting stolen," Monica finished. "But if Dylan gets caught, my Dad would probably murder him."

"Which wouldn't be a bad idea," Ziggy muttered.

"It may not be Dylan," Alan said. "Maybe it's his friends, and they're just storing the stolen goods here until they can sell them or something."

"But don't you see? If I tell Dad, then he'll have to go to the police, and there'll be a lot of publicity and people would laugh at him, and then Mother would leave for good." There was a stunned silence.

"Your parents are…" Josée said.

"Oh, it's a long story. The thing is, I know I should tell Dad, but should I wait until after this concert? Dad's organized the whole thing and put up the money and everything, and if there's suddenly police all over the place, it'll be a catastrophe."

"And it'll make your mother leave your dad?" Josée said.

"It'll be the last straw," Monica said. "I know it sounds stupid, but trust me. We may be a weird family, but at least we're together—not like most of the people at school, who have, like, twelve parents."

"Twelve?" Ziggy said.

"She's exaggerating," Alan said. He knew what she meant. He knew a lot of people with divorced parents. Josée was one of them.

"So why are you showing us this, then? If you already plan to tell?" Ziggy said.

"I had to tell somebody," Monica said.

"Could you find out if your brother is actually the one doing the break-ins?" Alan said. "If he's just storing the TVs and stuff, there wouldn't be that much trouble, would there?"

"I don't know," Monica said. "Maybe." She sounded miserable.

"We'll help," Josée said. She turned to the others. "Won't we?"

"How? We can't follow the Weem Team in the canoe—we're not allowed out past McGregor beach, remember?" Alan said.

"And they probably do the break-ins at night, right?" Ziggy said. "My curfew's at ten."

"Mine, too," Alan said.

"I have an idea," Josée said. "Your mother wanted you to make friends, right? Well, here we are. Why not ask if you can have a sleepover? All of us. We could spy on Dylan all night long."

Alan and Ziggy looked doubtfully at each other. A sleepover with girls?

"Come on, it would be great," Josée said. Monica was grinning.

"We could spend the day down here in the water," Monica said. "There's a water slide and everything—a diving board, too. Dylan would probably stay away during the day, but he always comes down here at night."

"And we could keep him under surveillance," Alan said, thoughtfully.

"I've always wanted to try a kayak," Ziggy said.

"Then it's settled," Monica said. "Great idea, Josée. Mother will say yes, I know it, and Dad won't care."

"Mamère is no problem," Josée said. "And Alain, your mother won't mind. She knows Mr. Weems from the Music Society, right? What about your grandfather, Zig?"

"He'll probably let me go," he said.

Just then, they heard a noise down below: a door slamming. Everybody froze.

"Quick—this way," Monica hissed, leaping for the light switch and turning it off, leaving them in semi-darkness. They emerged from the bedroom and quickly crossed the floor of the living room, eerily lit by moonlight from the big picture window. They crowded into another bedroom, this one with sliding glass door leading to a balcony. They could hear heavy feet coming up the stairs. Monica slid the glass door open and beckoned everybody out onto the balcony. There were stairs leading down into a clump of bushes beside the deck, the opposite side of the boathouse from the door they'd entered by. "Hurry—quiet!" Monica whispered. As they crept down the stairs, they saw the light come on in the room with the closet hiding place. As soon as they reached the ground, they ran as fast as they could all the way back up to the house.

When they got back to the patio, which was still crowded with partygoers, Monica, last in the line of runners, stopped suddenly and put her hand to her mouth. "Oh, no. I think I left the closet door open," she said.

"Alan Nearing, your mother's looking for you," a woman said, touching Alan's arm. It was Mrs. Brooks from the Music Society.

"Oh, hi, Mrs. Brooks. Thanks," he said. "I guess she wants to go, eh?"

Mrs. Brooks' mouth pursed, like she was sucking on a lemon. "I believe your sister's a trifle under the weather," she said.

"Her ankle again?"

"They're waiting by the front door, dear," was all she said. They all went together. Mrs. Nearing was hovering over Candace, who was sitting on the bench by the door again, as she had when they'd arrived. She looked ill.

"Sorry, Mom," he said. "We were down by the water. This is Monica Weems."

"Pleased to meet you, Monica," Mrs. Nearing said, but you could see she was distracted. "Alan, we need to get

Candace home soon. Her ankle's bothering her a bit—the one she twisted, you know, and I have a long day tomorrow as well. So I don't want to be too late. Did you have a good time?"

"Excellent," Alan said.

"Can Alan and his friends come for a sleepover tomorrow night?" Monica put in, right away. Alan would have liked to have choosen the moment a bit more carefully, but it was too late now. Mrs. Nearing frowned a little.

"I don't know, Monica. Perhaps, if your parents agree. We'll talk about it tomorrow, all right?"

"I'll ask Dad to call you," Monica said. They said their goodbyes at the door as Mrs. Nearing helped Candace to the van. She really did look unwell. Her ankle didn't look all that bad, though, Alan thought.

"Not a word about you-know-what," Monica said.

"I hope whoever that was didn't hear us," Josée said.

"I don't think they did. I waited for a second while you guys were running up the hill. Nobody came out. But if it was Dylan, he's sure to notice that the closet door was open."

"Will he know it was us?" Alan said.

"No way. He'll probably think it was one of the guests at the party, snooping around. He'll be scared, I bet."

"Maybe he'll move the stuff somewhere else, then," Alan said.

"I'll keep watch tonight. And I'll call you first thing tomorrow, okay? We're all in this together, right?"

"Right," Josée said. The boys nodded. Alan smiled to himself. The Alan Nearing Detective Agency now officially had its first case, he thought. He would be the youngest professional detective in history.

They got in the van. Candace was already strapped into the front seat, her head leaning against the window.

"Sorry about your ankle, Candace," Josée said, kindly, leaning forward.

"She shouldn't have done so much running around for Mr. Hugh Pratt," Alan said quietly to Ziggy. Candace whimpered, then suddenly opened the van door, leaned out and threw up all over the driveway.

Six

It was still dark when Alan got up the next morning. He and Ziggy and Josée had agreed to meet by the Community Centre next to the Kuskawa River and bike up to the Lookout to watch the sun come up. No special reason for it—it was just a cool thing to do.

Laingford was a busy place in the summer—tourists loved it. There were dozens of deep, cold lakes, hectares of rugged bush, and more resorts and campgrounds than you could count. By nine a.m. on most summer mornings, the downtown traffic was already heavy, local people heading to work and tourist people coming into town to get camping supplies, do banking, buy ice cream and generally just do tourist stuff.

Before the town woke up, though, it was a completely different place. Alan rode hands-free down Tannery Road, the long, steep hill that met Main Street at the lights by the post office. He made it all the way down without touching the handlebars—a first, and nobody was there to see, but it was satisfying anyway. At six a.m., Main Street was mostly deserted, except for a refrigerator truck unloading ice cream at the Treatstop, its open side door breathing white icy air onto the sidewalk, like an Arctic dragon. It was going to be a really hot day. The sky was already taking on a hazy look, with an electric blue coming through like the colour developing on a Polaroid photograph. Ziggy's grandfather had a Polaroid camera and let them use it sometimes, for special occasions. Alan stopped his bike for a moment beside the refrigerator truck to get some of the cold air. The delivery man came out of the store, wheeling a cart in front of him. He grinned at Alan.

"Yeah, guy, I know what you mean," he said. "Some days, I just wanna crawl in there and lock myself in."

"Sort of like your own personal air conditioner, eh?"

"'Zactly. Here, kid. Breakfast of champions." The man reached into a box beside the door and tossed him a package, which Alan caught, one-handed. It was a popsicle. An orange one. Perfect.

"Hey, thanks."

By the time he met up with Ziggy and Josée in front of the Community Centre, his mouth was orange, and he had an orange sploodge on the front of his white T-shirt. It was going to be a hot one, all right.

*   *   *

The Lookout in Laingford was built at the very top of a cliff overlooking the town. On a clear day, the view was amazing—almost like a vision of the town from a plane, each house and road looking small and neat, like a model railroad town, the cars and trees like toys. They were too late for the sunrise itself, but the sky was spectacular, even

50

so, red and orange clouds again, like the night before, with a darker blue above. All three of them were sweating already.

"You got a violin lesson today?" Ziggy called to Alan as they rode up the hill.

"Not till eleven. I haven't touched the thing since the last lesson, either, so there'll be trouble."

They were at the steepest part of the hill, and it was too hot to try and ride it. At least that's what Ziggy said when he got off his bike and started walking it. Josée and Alan did the same.

"Why don't you just tell your mom you want to quit?" Josée said.

"I don't know, really. She'd be mad, I guess."

"You could tell her that she's wasting her money paying for lessons you're not interested in," she said. "That usually works with mamère."

"Yeah, maybe."

"Didn't hearing Mr. Pratt play last night inspire you?" Ziggy asked.

"Nah. It probably inspired Candace, who's really good, you know—but me? I'll never be a great violin player, Zig. I don't have the ambition for it, for one thing. Candace is always practicing, but I hardly ever do."

"How *is* Candace?" Josée asked. After Candace had thrown up the night before, Mrs. Nearing had stopped pretending that it was her daughter's ankle that was the problem. They could all tell she had been drinking wine; she stank. Mrs. Nearing had powered down the van windows again and was really, really mad. She had dropped off Ziggy and Josée at their homes with hardly a word, and Alan had disappeared up to his bedroom as soon as he could and stayed there.

"She won't be up until noon, probably," he said. "I don't know."

"She'll have *la gueule de bois* all day," Josée said.

"Mouth of wood?" Ziggy said, after a moment.

"Yep. A hangover from drinking. My dad used to get them all the time." Alan and Ziggy knew that Josée's father hadn't been around for more than a year, but she didn't talk about him very much. They exchanged a look of surprise. "That smell in the van last night reminded me, that's all," she said. The look on her face said "end of subject".

"Well, I'm pretty sure my mom will ground Candace for the rest of her life," Alan said. "So she'll be able to practice even more than usual. Which will probably remind my mom that she hasn't heard me play in over a week."

"Well, you're gonna have to tell her some time," Ziggy said. "Tell her professional detectives don't play the violin."

"Sherlock Holmes played one," Alan said.

"Yeah, but he wasn't real," Josée said.

"I think I'll just wait for Mr. Ziegler to rip the instrument out of my hands and throw it at the wall," Alan said. "That could happen today, I guess."

"Hey, maybe that's where that drowned violin we found came from," Ziggy said. "Maybe Mr. Ziegler tossed somebody else's instrument into the lake because they wouldn't practice."

"Yeah, that was weird, eh? I was wondering about where it came from. I guess we'll never know, though, seeing as it sank to the bottom."

They had made it to the top. They wheeled their bikes out to the platform, built on the very edge of the cliff. Ziggy climbed up and sat on the railing, his feet dangling over.

"I wish you wouldn't do that," Alan said.

"Yeah, it gives me the heebies," Josée said.

Ziggy grinned. "You guys are just chicken," he said.

Alan ignored him. Ziggy wouldn't say that if he'd seen his hands-free coast down Tannery Road. They were looking down on the river, which spread beneath the cliff like a bright ribbon, meandering in smooth curves, already beginning to sparkle in the morning sun. Just coming in from the lake to the mouth of the river was a small wooden rowboat, with a tiny, hunched-over figure working the oars.

"Hey, look, there's Eubie," Alan said.

Eubie was one of the town's "characters", a man everybody knew, or at least recognized. Nobody called him Mr. Sadler. He was a sort of hermit who lived on a small island in the middle of Steamboat Lake—Sadler's Island, it was called. Ziggy's grandfather said Eubie owned the whole island, that it was worth a lot of money, but he lived there alone in a little hut. People had tried to get him to sell it, but he wouldn't. Eubie came in to town every so often for supplies, rowing his battered wooden boat slowly but steadily, ignoring the motor boats and passersby, his long white beard waving like a flag in the lake breeze. He didn't talk much, and he looked grumpy most of the time. Some of the little kids were scared of him, because he dressed in many layers, like an onion, and he wasn't very clean. Alan's mother called him "a harmless old man" and told the boys that they were on no account ever to tease him. They didn't, but others did.

"Uh-oh," Ziggy said. "Look what just came in at McGregor Beach." The beach, where they had dumped the canoe the day before, was right at the mouth of the Kuskawa River. Like a single hornet, a jet ski emerged from behind the point and came speeding towards Eubie's boat.

"I wonder what Dylan Weems is doing up so early?" Alan said. The distinctive yellow and black stripes of Dylan's jet ski were unmistakable.

Ziggy had brought a pair of binoculars with him, as he often did. Being a park ranger in the making, he was trying to learn about the Kuskawa wildlife and even carried a bird book around with him in his knapsack. His binocs were trained on the scene below.

"It's Dylan, all right. No sign of his gang, though."

"Dylan's probably even worse by himself," Alan said. "What's he going to do? Ram the old guy?"

"Nah—it looks like he's going to talk to him, actually." The jet ski had pulled alongside the rowboat and was holding steady, although even without binoculars Alan could see that Eubie had not stopped rowing.

"He's ignoring him," Josée said. *"Bonne chance."*

Then suddenly, Eubie stopped rowing, lifted an oar and hefted it into the air, turning it into an enormous weapon. Alan could see Dylan lean back in his seat and fumble with the controls of the jet ski, but before he could get away, the oar came down—not on Dylan's head, as they all thought for a moment, but directly on the nose of the jet ski. They could hear the yell Dylan made as the oar came down, heard the hollow thwack as it landed on the jet ski's fiberglass hull, the sounds bouncing off the sheer rock face of the cliff below the lookout, rising up as if the whole thing had been amplified.

"Wow," Ziggy and Josée said.

"That's gotta hurt," Alan said. "His dad's not going to be happy about that, if it made the kind of dent it sounded like."

"He had it coming," Ziggy said, with some satisfaction. "We should try that next time he tries to swamp us."

"I wonder what that was all about," Josée said. "It didn't look like he was trying to swamp Eubie—just talk to him." Dylan had by now got the jet ski started again and was racing back up the river to the lake. Eubie settled back down in his rowboat, replaced the oar he'd been swinging at Dylan and continued his journey.

"Who knows?" Ziggy said. "Maybe Dylan was trying to buy Sadler's Island with his burglar money."

"But this early in the morning? It was like he didn't want anyone to see, no? Maybe Eubie is mixed up in the cottage break-ins somehow," Josée said.

"Hey—maybe he's a fence," Alan said.

"A fence?"

"The person who sells stolen stuff for the robbers. It's what they call them."

"Well, if he *is* a fence," Josée said, "it looks like there's no deal with the robbers this time. He looked pretty mad."

Ziggy got off the railing and walked to the end of the platform so he could watch the last of Eubie as he rowed around the bend in the river. "Another mystery," he said in a dramatic voice. "That's three cases for the Alan Nearing Detective Agency, eh? The drowned violin, the stolen goods in Monica's boathouse and now this."

"Maybe they're connected," Josée said.

"That reminds me," Ziggy said. "Are we going to be able to do this overnight at Monica's, after your lesson this afternoon? Vati said it would be okay if I went. I asked him this morning."

"Mamère said I could go, too, as long as she could talk to Monica's parents first."

"So I guess we just have to find out if Monica was able to fix it," Alan said. "Although my mom may not let me if Mr. Ziegler goes ballistic at the lesson and calls her or something. I can see me now, grounded for the rest of the summer, chained to the violin and locked in my room."

"Yeah—with Candace," Ziggy said.

"That would be child abuse," Josée said. "We'd have to call the Children's Aid."

"No, the murder squad," Alan said.

"Mr. Nearing, you are seriously conflicted about this issue, aren't you?" Ziggy said, doing his impression of Ms. Keppler, the school board counselling lady. "Maybe you should talk to a trusted adult about it."

"Oh, ha ha," Alan said, not really laughing. But on the way back down the hill, he wondered if he might need counselling for real before he got up enough nerve to tell his mom he wanted to quit violin.

* * *

A couple of hours later, Alan was in his room, collecting his sheet music and checking inside his violin case to make sure the bow was okay. He really *hadn't* gone near the instrument for a week, and if he'd forgotten to loosen the bow-tension after the last lesson, the bow would be ruined by now. Then, even if Alan didn't admit it right away, Mr. Ziegler would know he hadn't practiced.

He heard the phone ring downstairs and found himself hoping that it was his violin teacher calling to cancel the lesson for some reason. But there was no reassuring "Alan! It's for you!" from below, so his hopes went right out the window. Maybe it was Monica's mother, calling about the overnight. Probably, though, it someone calling for Candace, as usual. Maybe it was Mr. Pratt, asking her to come in and be his personal maid again. It was ten thirty, and there had been no sound yet from her room. He resisted the urge to run around in the upstairs hallways, stomping his feet and slamming doors.

Mrs. Nearing was just putting the phone down as he entered the kitchen. Her face was worried, and Alan wondered if the caller had, after all, been Mr. Ziegler.

"Alan, that was the police," she said. "They want to question you, Candace, Ziggy and Josée this morning—well, they're questioning everybody who was at the party last night."

"What? Why?"

"They found Hugh Pratt unconscious on the patio this morning. He's in the hospital now, with a severe concussion, and apparently the Stradivarius is missing."

Seven

I know that you were all at home when this incident occurred," the police officer said. She had arranged to meet all the young people at the Nearings' house just before lunch. Mrs. Nearing had called Mr. Ziegler to cancel Alan's violin lesson. Yes, it was awful news about the violin and Mr. Pratt, but it was like a get-out-of-jail-free card, and he felt glad, secretly, inside. His bow had been fine, but it would have been awful, even so.

Mrs. Nearing asked to be present during the police officer's visit, but she had to promise not to interfere with the questioning. The officer's name was Constable Mills, with the Laingford OPP detachment, and she went to some trouble at the beginning to reassure Alan, Candace, Ziggy and Josée that they themselves weren't under suspicion for the theft of the violin or the assault on Mr. Pratt. The crimes had been committed, the police knew, long after they were all at home and in bed.

"But we often find that young people are far more observant than their adult counterparts," Constable Mills, said with a smile. "Now, this crime may very well be a random act—maybe somebody broke in to the Weems's home looking for something to steal—we don't know yet."

"But Mr. Pratt was found unconscious on the patio, wasn't he?" Alan said.

"Yes, that's right. We don't know what he was doing there. According to the family, they all went to bed at around two in the morning, after the party ended, so he must have got up again."

"He was drinking a lot of wine," Candace said, suddenly. "Maybe he fell over and hit his head." Alan had wondered if Candace was going to say anything at all. She had come downstairs after their mom went up to tell her what had happened, and she *did* look like she had a mouth (or a head) made of wood, like Josée had said. He had asked if the police would know that Candace had been drinking underage, and whether she could get arrested. Candace had given him a poisonous look, but Mrs. Nearing had just said not to be so silly. Still, Candace had been sitting with her arms crossed, looking angry and sick and not saying a word until now.

"Oh, yes?" Constable Mills said. "You noticed that, did you? Was he behaving badly?" Alan wondered if Candace would say that she had got a glass of wine for him at the bar. That wouldn't be a good idea, judging from the look on his mom's face. Maybe Candace had got him more than one, and maybe got herself some, too. Not a thing to tell a police officer, unless you wanted to go to jail.

"Now, Candace—it was a party," Mrs. Nearing said. "People drink wine at parties."

The police officer held up her hand. "Please, Mrs. Nearing," she said. "Go on, Candace."

"I know he was drinking a lot of wine, because I was sort of helping him, carrying his briefcase—like his personal assistant? He asked me to. I wasn't following him around or anything."

"That's helpful," the officer said. "So you were near him all evening, were you?"

"Most times. Unless he asked me to get something for him."

"Like what did you get?"

Alan tensed. Here it comes, he thought. Candace gets arrested.

"Like his violin—for when he played for everybody."

His mother broke in again. "Constable, this can't have anything to do with the theft of the violin. Everybody saw him play it, after Candace retrieved it for him. It hadn't disappeared at that point. You said yourself it happened after two in the morning, when the kids were all home."

The officer turned to her. "Yes, but now we know for sure your daughter handled the violin, you see. So if we get it back and find her fingerprints on it, we'll be able to eliminate them right away."

Candace squeaked. "I'm a suspect?" she said.

The officer smiled. "Of course not, Candace. Don't worry. But you're an important source of information. You all are. Really, you should relax, Mrs. Nearing."

"Yeah, Mom," Alan said. They would have to take Candace's fingerprints. How cool was that?

"I handled the violin, too," he said. "When I carried it in from the van, remember you guys?" Ziggy and Josée nodded.

60

"I did, too," Ziggy said. "I sort of touched it after you picked it up, right? So did you, Josée."

"Well, maybe you could all come down to Headquarters later, and we'll take your prints, okay?" Constable Mills said. "No rush—just some time in the next couple of days."

"Sweet," Ziggy said.

"Now, one last question," the officer said. "Did any of you see anything last night at the party that you think was suspicious? Someone threatening Mr. Pratt, maybe? Strangers lurking around in the bushes, who didn't look like they were part of the party?"

Alan couldn't tell if she was joking or not. It was such a TV line: "Did you see anything suspicious?" And they all had—they'd seen the hidden stuff in the boathouse. They'd also seen the violin player, Annette, have a fight with Mr. Pratt right out in public. Maybe she'd hit him on the head and stolen the violin. She had looked mad enough.

"There was a lady who was pretty mad at him," Candace said. Her eyes were gleaming suddenly in a not-very-nice way.

"Oh, yes?" the officer said.

"Candace, don't exaggerate," Mrs. Nearing said. "She exaggerates," she added to the constable.

"I do not, Mom," Candace said. "This lady was practically yelling at him. Then she bumped into me, and I was carrying the violin, and I almost dropped it. She called him names and everything."

"It's true. We saw that, too," Alan said.

"Do you know who it was?" Constable Mills asked.

Alan didn't want to say, but he was annoyed with Candace for getting all the attention. He was supposed to be the detective, not her. Anyway, plenty of people saw the confrontation, so it wasn't like he was telling a secret.

"Her name is Annette, I think," he said. "She's one of the orchestra players." His mother made a little *tsk* sound, but Alan pretended not to hear it. At least he wasn't going to spill the beans about the boathouse closet. That was a real secret, at least until the Alan Nearing Detective Agency did some investigating. They'd promised Monica they wouldn't tell.

"Maybe we'll talk to her, then," Constable Mills said, standing up as if to go. "By the way, what happened to the violin after he finished playing it? He performed for everybody, you said, Candace ? Did he keep it with him, or did he ask you to put it back in his room?"

"We both put it back," Candace said. "I mean—he gave it to me after he finished playing and asked me to put it—yes, in his room. He ended up coming too, though, because he needed to get something. People kept stopping us, talking to him, and Mr. Weems wanted to see the violin, so I sort of held the case."

"Like she was a rack of comics," Alan muttered to the others.

"Yeah, like the violin was a new *Spiderman* issue," Ziggy said, grinning.

"So the last time you saw it, the violin was put in his room. Did he lock the door?" the officer said. Her eyes had gone sort of narrow and glinty.

"Yes. It was one of those old fashioned locks with a

key, and he took it out and put it in his pocket. He made a big thing of locking it, because Mr. Weems came too, and Mr. Pratt apologized, saying he knew everybody was honest, but he had to be careful. Mr. Weems said 'Don't lose that key—it's the only one there is,' and then we went back to the party."

"So that means the violin was stolen right from his room, past a locked door?" Alan said. It sounded like one of those five-minute-mysteries.

"Exactly, Alan. You're analytical, aren't you?" the officer said. "We could use you on the force." Alan felt his face getting red, but he didn't care. "Police Chief Nearing" would sound pretty good, he thought.

Nobody said much more, and the police officer got up to go, suggesting that they call if they thought of anything else. "Ask for me when you come to the station for fingerprints, okay? I'll take you on a tour."

"I liked her," Alan said, after she left.

"One good thing about all this—getting questioned by the police and all that," Ziggy said, "is that you missed your violin lesson, eh?"

"And of course, before next week, you're going to practice like crazy, right?" Josée said. She sounded just a little sarcastic, Alan thought.

"Yeah, right," he said. "I'm still holding out for something horrible to happen to my instrument."

Ziggy grinned. "Yeah, maybe you should lend it to Hugh Pratt and see if he can't get that stolen as well," he said.

*   *   *

After lunch, Monica's mother called Mrs. Nearing to arrange the overnight. Ziggy and Josée were still there, and after some more phone calls back and forth, it was all settled. Monica had pulled it off. Not only that, but somehow the three of them had managed to convince Mrs. Nearing that it would be less complicated, transportation-wise, if they went to the Weems's place in Ziggy's canoe.

"Maybe she was distracted by the violin thing," Josée said, when they were alone.

"That and Candace," Alan said.

"She did say it would make her day easier, getting us out from underfoot," Ziggy added.

"That bugs me so much—*underfoot,*" Alan said. "Yes. The rehearsal's tonight, and she's one of the organizers. I guess she has enough to think about. This has really worked out."

They agreed to meet down at the dock where Ziggy's canoe was kept in an hour. Ziggy and Josée went home to collect their stuff, and Alan stayed well out of the way of his mother, in case she suddenly changed her mind. But she didn't, and she drove him down to the dock to see them off.

"Now I know the Weems' house is only just around on the edge of the bay, so it's not far from McGregor Beach," she said. "If it was any further out, I wouldn't let you go. I'm still not sure this is a good idea."

Their knapsacks were in the canoe, their lifejackets were on and they were ready to go. Mrs. Nearing stood beside them on the end of the dock, looking worried. Alan remembered when Monica had muttered at the party how she hated it when her dad spoke in public. Well, there were times when his mother's concern drove him crazy, too.

"Call and leave a message as soon as you get there, all right?" she said. "I know I can trust all of you to be responsible and safe. It's not a long journey, but I won't be happy until I know you've arrived."

"We'll be *fine,* Mom," Alan finally said.

"You're only eleven, Alan."

"Twelve next month," he said.

Ziggy put on his fake school principal voice. "We young people are the future, you know," he said. "You can count on us, Mrs. Nearing." Then he saluted, and they all cracked up.

"Off you go, then," Mrs. Nearing said, hugged each of them as if they were going on a journey to the Arctic, then let them go.

"She's still there," Josée said, a minute later, looking back from her middle position as they paddled gently down the river.

"We'll be around the bend in a second, and then she'll go," Alan said from the bow. "She said she has a million things to do today. She'll forget about us after a while. You'll see—I'll call, and she'll say 'Alan who?'"

"You're lucky she won't let you have a cell phone," Ziggy said from the stern. "She'd make you call every ten minutes. I bet Monica's got one."

"Two," Josée said. "One's so small it looks like a gum card."

"So she can talk to herself?" Ziggy said. "You said she didn't have any friends."

"She has us, now," Josée said firmly.

It was a bright, calm Thursday. There wasn't much boat traffic on the river, and it was very quiet. Near McGregor Beach, they stopped to watch a duck and a gaggle of ducklings poke about in the reeds growing along the shoreline.

"I really hope the Weem Team isn't around," Josée said.

"Mother ducks are smart," Ziggy said. "Dylan's jet ski can't come in this far without getting stuck. See how shallow the bottom is? That's why she's herding them away from the deep water, see?"

"We should stick close to shore ourselves," Alan said. "For the same reason."

They paddled past the beach and out into the bay. The top windows of the Weems mansion could just be seen through the trees to the right, on the point of land where the bay opened out into Steamboat Lake. There was no sign of any jet skis, just bright, smooth reflecting water, a slight breeze and the hot sun in a pure blue sky. Perfect.

"If we keep to the shore on this side again, we'll be there in less than five minutes," Ziggy said, steering them in the direction of a small red boathouse and dock halfway along the bay. This was the way they had come the day before, to check out an interesting marshy place just before the point, where they had found the drowned violin.

"Monica said she'd wait for us in a kayak," Josée said. "We won't be able to see her from here, though."

"We have to get closer to the point," Alan said.

As they paddled past the red boathouse, someone called out to them from the dock.

It was Eubie, his arm raised, beckoning them over.

"Your parents don't have a motor boat nearby, do they?" he called, when they'd paddled in a little closer. "I lost an oar back in town and thought I could paddle home with just the one, but I got to feeling a little woozy and had to stop. I'd appreciate a tow to my place—it's on that island out there." They looked. Sadler's Island was very rocky, with a covering of trees like thick fur. It didn't look like there was any house on it, but maybe it was on the other side.

Alan had never heard Eubie say more than a few words. He sounded like a normal person, no matter what people might say about him.

"We're going somewhere where they have motor boats," Ziggy said. "We could tow you there, and you could get a ride home that way."

"Is it far?" he said. "You kids are kind of small."

"It's just on the point there," Josée said, pointing. The old man frowned.

"Not *that* place," he said. "I'm not getting help from him." His voice was not normal, all of a sudden. It was really angry.

"Well, that's where we're supposed to be going, sir," Ziggy said, as politely as he could. "Do you want us to call someone?"

"Nobody to call," he said. "Unless the marine patrol, and I don't want them round my place just now." He gave them a sharp look.

"How strong *are* you?" he said. They all sat up straighter

in their seats. Alan exchanged looks with the others. Could they tow him across to the island? It wasn't that far, really, but it would be open water, where the wind was stronger, and the waves were bigger. He could see that both his friends were willing to try. Monica would be looking out for them, probably, and they'd be seen once they got out far enough, so she would know they were taking a side trip.

"Strong enough," Alan said. "Throw us a rope and we'll try, anyway."

Eight

Once they picked up speed, it didn't feel like they were towing a rowboat with an adult aboard at all. But after they got outside the shelter of the shore, it turned into hard work. The breeze, which had felt like nothing close to shore, turned into a real wind in the middle of the bay.

"Whatever you do, don't stop paddling," Ziggy called out to the others. "If we lose speed, we'll never get started again."

Luckily, the canoe was riding quite low in the water, so that the wind didn't make much difference to the steering. Ziggy and Alan had once been caught in the canoe in a big wind on Mud Lake and had kept getting blown off course, but that wasn't happening this time. It just felt like they were pushing against a giant, unseen hand. Ziggy started counting strokes out loud to keep them paddling all at the same time.

"*Stroke*, two, three, four, *Stroke,* two, three, four!" he barked, like a sergeant in the army.

Slowly, with what seemed to be three paddle-strokes forward for every two inches gained, they made it into the lee of the island, and the wind died suddenly, as if someone had turned off a switch.

"Man, you're a slave-driver," Alan said to Ziggy, grinning because they had made it. "Next time, why not hire a guy with a kettle drum and a whip?"

"Great job, Captain," Mr. Sadler called from the rowboat. It didn't seem right at all to call him Eubie any more. He moved forward to untie his boat from the canoe. "I can take her from here, I reckon."

"Are you still feeling woozy?" Josée said. "We can take you right to your dock, you know."

"Well," the old man said, hesitating. "I suppose you can. I'm not being very grateful, am I? You'll be wanting a rest and a drink of water, too."

"We *should* start back right away, but I think I need a rest first," Alan said. The others probably did too, he figured, and it would be dumb if nobody said so, and they ended up tipping the canoe over just because they were tired. "And we should maybe call the Weems place to say we'll be late." He'd forgotten that the old man didn't seem to be a friend of Mr. Weems. Mr. Sadler's face darkened again.

"No phone," he said. "Sorry. If you paddle round the corner there, you'll see my mooring."

Instead of a dock, Mr. Sadler had a wharf—a wall, built out into the water. They paddled over to it, and Mr. Sadler untied his rowboat from the canoe and moored it to a metal ring set in the wall. There were groceries and supplies stored in the bottom of the boat, and he piled them out onto the wharf, then climbed out himself. He was about to say something to them when suddenly his face went white, and he clutched at his upper arm like it was hurting him. He swayed a little on his feet.

"Dang," he said. "I gotta lie down." He seemed to forget they were there, and turning like he was half asleep, walked dazedly along the wharf and onto a narrow path leading off into the trees.

"Mr. Sadler, are you okay?" called Josée, but there was no reply. They waited for a moment, listening. "We can't just leave," Josée said. "Not until we're sure he's okay. He looked like he was going to keel over."

"There's no phone, remember?" Ziggy said. "What are we going to do if he has a heart attack or something? You know CPR?"

"Actually, yes," Josée said curtly. "So do you—it was on our canoe course, M'sieu Smartypants."

"I'm not putting my mouth anywhere near him," Ziggy said.

"He's left his supplies on the wharf, there," Alan said. "We could take them up for him—make sure he's not dying or anything."

"Please let him not be dying," Ziggy said.

They pulled the canoe up onto a pebbly beach area and picked up the packages Mr. Sadler had left on the wharf. Several cloth grocery bags were full of produce, there was a bag of potatoes and a big jug of drinking water. They divided up the load and set off in the direction the old man had taken.

The path was steep and overgrown, and they couldn't see much for the first few moments. Then a wooden staircase appeared, leading upward. They could see the edge of a porch and some railing through the trees.

"What if he has a dog?" Ziggy said.

"We'd hear barking by now if he did," Alan said. "Maybe a cat, though. He looks like he could be a cat person." At the top of the staircase, a clearing opened up, and there was the house. It was like a house in a little kids' storybook. Wooden, with a tiny, cleanly-swept porch.

"C'est adorable," Josée said. Alan wondered why people always referred to Eubie Sadler's place as a "shack". He wondered if anybody had actually ever been there to see it, or if a legend about the old man had just built up over the years—something totally inaccurate and mean. The place was small, certainly. Wood-sided, grey and weathered, but it looked water-tight. The roof had clean new shingles, and a shiny metal chimney poked up through it. One of the two front windows was broken, but had been carefully repaired, quite recently, it looked like, with freshly-cut boards nailed across it.

"Cool," Ziggy said. "It's like the witch's house in Hansel and Gretel."

"No witch, though," Alan said. "Just Mr. Sadler."

They called out, but got no answer, so they moved forward, very quietly.

The front door wasn't locked. Alan knocked, waited, then pushed the door open slowly, in case there *was* a dog, a big, silent one that liked to wait until the unsuspecting intruder was inside and unable to escape. No dog, but the interior was a huge contrast to the neat appearance of the outside. Pictures had been smashed, furniture broken, curtains torn from the windows. It looked like a cyclone had hit.

"Holy cow. Somebody's trashed the place," Ziggy said.

"Somebody did, indeed," said Mr. Sadler from behind them. He had come in from outside, and was looking much better, now. "It's kind of you to bring my things up, kids," he said. "You want some water before you go?" It was clear he wasn't comfortable with a houseful of people.

"We thought you were sick," Josée said. "We wanted to make sure you were okay."

"Much obliged," the old man said and sat down on the only chair they could see that wasn't broken. "I took one of my pills—I'll be fine in a few minutes."

"Did this just happen? When you were out in the boat?" Alan asked, gesturing at the mess.

"No, it was a couple of days ago," he said. "I just haven't got around to cleaning it up yet. Pardon the mess." He seemed really embarrassed about it, Alan thought.

"Did you call the police?" he asked. "There have been other break-ins around the lake, you know."

"I know," Mr. Sadler said, and that was all. They all gazed for a moment at the walls, where an ugly, obscene message had been sprayed in red paint.

"Oh, man, Mr. Sadler," Ziggy said. "This is terrible."

"Yep. And I've got my suspicions about who did it, but I'm not going to the police," he said. "No point. It's not the end of the world. A lick of paint over that, and you'd never know it was there."

"You'd remember, though," Josée said. There was a silence as they all thought about that. It was true. There were some things you couldn't cover up with paint.

"I'll get you a drink of water, kids, then you'd best be on your way," Mr. Sadler said, after a moment, and went to the kitchen.

Alan was looking more closely at some of the pictures that had survived the vandalism. One was an old newspaper article with a picture in a frame, yellowed but still readable. In it, a young man in a suit was standing at an old-fashioned microphone, playing a violin, an orchestra in the background. The musician looked vaguely familiar.

"Is that Mr. Pratt?" Alan said, pointing.

"No way," Ziggy said. "Look at the date at the top: 1945. Mr. Pratt wasn't even born then." Before they had a chance to read the article, Mr. Sadler was back with three glasses of water on a tray.

"Cool glasses," Josée said. They were tall and heavy, sort of frosted, as if they'd been in the freezer, though they weren't cold. On each glass, glittery gold lettering read "Keewin Inn", with a silhouette of a dancing couple in glittery black, under a crescent moon.

"Only the best for company," Mr. Sadler said. "The water's fresh, too. Drink up." They did and put the glasses back on the tray, which Mr. Sadler was still holding.

"So—you're feeling okay now, right?" Josée said to him.

"Just fine, missy, thanks for asking. I'll have a nap, and be right as rain in no time. I thank you all kindly for towing me home."

"You're welcome," they said.

74

"Just one favour more, if you don't mind," he said. "I'd appreciate it if you didn't tell anybody about the mess here. Or about coming here at all. I don't like visitors, as a rule, though I'd make an exception in your case."

"We won't tell," Alan said.

"I don't want people to think that I'm at home to strangers," Mr. Sadler said. He was getting grumpy again and was herding them towards the door.

"We understand, Mr. Sadler," Alan said. "We're going now."

"We hope you feel better soon," Josée said.

On the way back down the wooden stairs, Ziggy, who was first in line, looked back at the others.

"I sure am glad we didn't have to perform CPR on that guy," he said. Just then they heard it. Coming from the cabin, back in the trees, a melancholy sound, which at first sounded like someone moaning. They stopped, thinking Mr. Sadler was calling for help—maybe he was woozy again. Then the moan became a sad tune, a lament, played softly on a violin.

"Is that a recording?" Ziggy said.

The music was stronger now, as if the player had forgotten that there were people around. The sound was like warm honey, like a human voice. "No, it's him," Alan said. "And it sounds like he's playing the Stradder."

Nine

They had not gone back to see if Mr. Sadler was really playing the Stradder, mostly because Ziggy and Josée didn't believe it when Alan said he could tell by the sound.

"You're crazy," Ziggy said.

"He didn't want to go near the Weems place, remember?" Josée added. "You think he stole it? I think Dylan and his gang took it."

"Maybe they sold it to him," Alan said.

"Yeah—like it was obvious Dylan and Mr. Sadler were best friends when we saw them on the river this morning," Ziggy said sarcastically.

"Well, it sure sounded like the Stradder to me," Alan said.

The wind was behind them on the way back across the bay, and it only took them a few minutes to return to the lee of the shore, just before the point. There was a kayak bobbing in the water near the marshy place they'd been the day before. It was Monica, and she raised her double paddle at them as they sped towards her.

"I saw you guys out there from our beach," she said when they got close enough to talk. "Were you over on

Sadler's Island? Did the old man chase you off? He did that to us, once."

"We towed him over, actually," Alan said. "He lost an oar and was sort of stranded."

"Wow—that must have been a hard paddle," she said.

"Sans blague," Josée said. "But we got to see his place —it's really neat."

"You said he lost an oar? There's one in the water over there," Monica said. "I thought it was one of ours, and I was going to ask you to tow it back. I can't in this thing."

The kayak was small, with only room for one person's legs, and there was no rope attached to it. The kayak paddle had blades at both ends, like a double spoon, and needed both hands.

"Look at that," Ziggy said. "If he'd let us tow him to your place, we would have found it before we got there, and he could have rowed *himself* home."

"Except that he was woozy," Josée said. "He would have conked out in the middle of the bay."

"So that belongs to the old man?" Monica said. They looked at it, bobbing there, caught in some reeds. It didn't look like it had been there for long—it wasn't waterlogged yet. "I wonder how it got here."

"We should return it, I guess," Alan said. "Mr. Sadler won't be able to go anywhere with only one oar."

"Not now, though," Ziggy said. "I'll have a woozy-attack myself if I have to paddle all the way back there again." The others agreed. Besides, Monica said her mother was waiting for them back at the house and wanted to take them all into town for ice cream.

"I know you just got here, but Mother insisted," she said.

"Ice cream sounds great," Ziggy said. "I never say no to ice cream." The others agreed.

*　　*　　*

Alan called home as soon as they got to the Weems's boathouse. Monica had her cell phone with her ("Mother likes to keep track of me," she said) and handed it to him. As he had expected, there was no answer, and he had to leave a message.

"Hi, Mom. We're here and we're fine, so you can stop worrying now," he said. "We're going for ice cream. Um... I hope the rehearsal goes okay. Bye." He handed the cell phone back. "There. She won't know what time I called, and as far as she knows we came right here and didn't go anywhere near the island, okay everybody?"

"Why the big secret?" Monica asked. On the way up to the house, they told her about the mess in Eubie Sadler's cabin.

"You think it was Dylan, don't you?" she said. "So do I." Alan couldn't resist adding his theory that Mr. Sadler somehow had got hold of the missing Stradder.

"We think Alan's just got violins on the brain," Ziggy said.

"Isn't it more likely that Dylan and his gang stole it?" Monica said.

"That's what we thought," Josée said.

"What do the police think?" Alan said. "They must

have been swarming all over the place here. Are they still here?"

"No swarm," Monica said, "just a couple of policemen, and they didn't stay very long." They had reached the stone patio, which looked even bigger in daylight—no sign of the party from the night before, except that the giant gas barbecue was being cleaned by a man in overalls.

"This is Justin, everybody," Monica said. "He's our caretaker and security guy. Justin, these are my friends who are staying overnight, so don't worry if you see us sneaking around, eh?"

Justin was an older man who looked like he worked out. He didn't look very happy, Alan thought, but maybe it was because he was cleaning a barbecue. His hands were smeared with black, and there was a greasy bucket of water beside him. He gave them a dirty look and grunted.

"Dad sort of blamed Justin for the violin thing, I think," Monica whispered as they headed into the house. "He was in Dad's study for a long time with the police and was still there after they left."

"Bummer for him," Ziggy said. "You think he was in on it?"

"No way," Monica said. "He's really nice—he's just in a bad mood right now, that's all. I would be, too. My dad can be pretty scary when he wants to be. That's why this thing with Dylan—if he's the robber, is going to be just awful."

"Surely, though, with the violin gone, the police are going to search the place and find that other stuff, and it'll all come out," Alan said.

"Maybe, but they haven't searched anything so far,"

Monica said. "And I sneaked up to the boathouse closet before getting the kayak out. Dylan's out jet skiing with his friends, and it's all still there. And no violin—it was the first thing I looked for."

"Maybe Dylan and his friends are selling the Stradder right now—to some fences," Josée said.

"Huh?" Monica said, but before they could explain, Mrs. Weems appeared, clucking like a mother hen and herded them all into the PT Cruiser parked out front.

Introductions were made, everybody shook hands, then, as Mrs. Weems started the car, the questioning began.

"Now, I've spoken to all your parents—well, guardians —on the phone, so they all know that you'll be well looked after," she said. She spoke clearly and precisely, like a teacher. She looked a bit like one, too, although Alan thought that no teacher he knew would wear a bright yellow pantsuit to school. She wore lots of jewellery—gold and silver bracelets that jangled whenever she moved her hands. "I know your mother, Alan," she went on. "Mary-Anne and I have been on the Society's organizing committee together for years. And I knew your father, of course." Alan's father, a photojournalist, had disappeared in Haiti when Alan was a baby. It was one reason Alan wanted to be a detective. One day, he was going to find out what had happened.

Mrs. Weems continued. "But Ziggy, I've never met your grandfather. What's his background?"

Ziggy squirmed in the back seat. "He used to be an engineer," he said. "He, um, drives a cab, now."

"That's nice. And you live with him, do you?"

80

"My parents are entymologists," Ziggy said. "That means they study bugs. They're away a lot. In the Amazon, right now."

"That's interesting," she said. "Do they ever take you with them on their trips?"

"Sometimes," Ziggy said. The fact that the Breuers, his parents, had left Ziggy behind while they got to paddle down the Amazon river was still a sore point with him. They had been gone for six months already, and Ziggy didn't like to talk about it.

"And Ziggy—that's short for…?"

"Sigmund," Ziggy muttered.

"That's unusual," Mrs. Weems said, brightly, and moved on. "And Josée—that's French, dear, isn't it?"

Alan resisted the urge to go "du'uh." He wasn't sure he liked Monica's mother.

"Yes, I was born in Quebec," Josée said. "Mamère and I moved here last year. She works at the prison in Wenonah."

"That's…nice," Mrs. Weems said. They had arrived on Main Street, and Mrs. Weems stopped talking while she concentrated on fitting the PT Cruiser into a tiny spot just outside the Treatstop. "Well, we're here!" she said. "You kids go in and order anything you want. I just have to drop in to the jewellery shop for a moment, and I'll join you presently. Tell them I'll pay for it. We can eat inside where it's cool and talk some more." Off she went, in a cloud of perfume and jangling bracelets, leaving them standing on the sidewalk.

"Sorry about that," Monica said, her face red. "Mother

likes to interview people, for some reason."

"You think we passed?" Josée said.

"Absolument," Monica said, grinning. "Come on, I feel like a triple hot fudge sundae. Mother's paying."

They all had sundaes. Ziggy chose three different flavours of ice-cream in his: rum and raisin, wildberry ripple and tiger stripe. On top, he asked for two sauces (hot fudge and marshmallow) plus sprinkles, M&Ms and whipped cream.

"I feel woozy just *looking* at that, Zig," Josée said, when his creation was handed across the counter. She ordered chocolate ice cream with butterscotch sauce on hers.

"How come you're not, like, way fat?" Monica asked Ziggy.

"I have a speedy metabolism, my Vati says," Ziggy said.

"You're lucky," Monica said. She ordered two small scoops of vanilla ice cream with fruit on top.

"I thought you wanted a triple hot fudge one?" Alan said.

"That's what I *wanted,*" Monica said. "But Mother keeps track of everything I eat, and I'd be in trouble."

"Why? You're not fat," Josée said.

"I know, but I could be, she says. She was a real lardo when she was a girl. I've seen pictures. She doesn't want me to go through what she went through."

Alan's sundae wasn't quite as elaborate as Ziggy's, although he chose two flavours of ice cream—chocolate peanut butter and cookie dough. He had crushed Skor bars on top and considered it perfect.

Mrs. Weems had arrived, and after paying for the sundaes, she came over and joined them at their table by the window. She had a baby-cone of vanilla, which she held with the tips of her polished fingernails. When her tongue darted out to lick it, Alan thought she looked exactly like Lizzie the lizard, their Grade Five classroom pet.

"Now, I'm so glad you're all going to be able to keep Monica company tonight," she said. "Giles and I will be at the rehearsal for the concert, of course, and we were wondering what to do with her." Alan remembered how his own mother had told them she was happy to have them out from underfoot. He rolled his eyes at Monica, who rolled hers back.

"We'll be back quite late, so we probably won't see you," Mrs. Weems went on. "But of course there's plenty of room for guests, and the housekeeper is there if you need anything. Clearly you won't need much to eat, after this. I hope you're not going to finish *all* of that, Monica, dear."

"I'm done," Monica said, putting her spoon down.

"Speaking of guests," Alan said, "is there even going to *be* a rehearsal tonight? Didn't Mr. Pratt get knocked on the head, and isn't he in hospital? And what's he going to play on? Unless the police find the Stradder this afternoon." Mrs. Weems laughed—a tinkling sound, like her bracelets made.

"Oh, you're sweet. Quite the detective, aren't you?" she said. "Well, the police seem to think that the violin will turn up in one of the pawn shops in town—a local job, you might say. It's terrible, of course, but we're not going to panic yet. And Mr. Pratt is fine, just a bit of a headache, poor boy, but he's back home with us, now, and he fully intends to go on with the rehearsal. He's borrowing a violin from one of the orchestra members."

"So somebody else doesn't get to play?" Alan said. "That's a bummer."

"Hey, you could lend him yours," Ziggy said.

"I don't think mine would impress him," Alan said. "It's no Stradder."

"That's a sweet thought though, Alan," Mrs. Weems said. "I'll tell him you offered, shall I? He'll be tickled." Alan wasn't sure he wanted to tickle Mr. Pratt, but he nodded anyway. The rest of them had finished their ice cream. Ziggy picked up his bowl and licked it, which made Josée and Monica giggle, especially when they saw the look on Mrs. Weems's face. Alan knew that Ziggy had been eyeing Monica's leftovers, too.

"Thank you very kindly for that, ma'am," Ziggy said to Mrs. Weems, bowing his head and doing his grandfather impression. "I'll just finish off Monica's sundae, here, and will not need feeding again until we go back to school in the fall." Monica grinned and pushed her bowl over to him.

"That reminds me, kids, we have to take a quick side trip before we go back home," Mrs. Weems said. "I have to drop something off at the Pioneer Museum and meet with the director for a few moments. Maybe you could look around a bit while you're waiting. There's a new display that you might find quite educational."

"Mo*ther,*" Monica said. "It's the summer."

"What? There's something wrong with education in the summer," Mrs. Weems said, raising an eyebrow.

"We don't mind, Mrs. Weems," Alan said. "I like the museum." He nudged Ziggy in the ribs. Ziggy's mouth was totally stuffed with vanilla ice cream at that moment, but he nodded and made "uh-huh" noises.

Later, on the way back out to the car, Alan whispered to the others. "Bear with me," he said. "I've just remembered something and I think we should check it out."

"What? Check what out? At the museum?" Ziggy said.

"Uh-huh. I've just remembered where I've seen those glasses before—the ones that Mr. Sadler gave us to drink water out of. There are some exactly like it in one of the displays."

"So? That would just mean that Mr. Sadler owns some antiques, wouldn't it?" Josée said. "You're not still trying to turn him into a robber, are you?"

"We'll see," Alan said. "Wouldn't it be interesting if the glasses at the museum had disappeared, just like the Stradder?"

Ten

The Kuskawa Pioneer Museum was set on a forty-acre piece of land next to Lookout Hill. It was a whole village, really, not just a museum. There were lots of old-fashioned buildings. Some had even been picked up and moved by truck from where they were originally. There were houses, a general store, a schoolhouse, an inn, a blacksmith's shop and lots of farm animals. People walked around in costume pretending to be pioneers, making candles and soap and feeding the chickens, and you could join in yourself, if you wanted to. Alan, Ziggy and Josée had been there dozens of times, usually on school trips. The best time to go was near dark, when it got a little bit spooky. They always went at Hallowe'en.

The museum displays were kept in an old community hall building. Inside, it was all shiny wood—floors, walls and ceiling, and the sun blazed in the big windows. It was echoey and hot and smelled of furniture polish and old things. There were all sorts of displays set up about life in pioneer Kuskawa, with old logging equipment and clothing, machines and old-fashioned toys. Ziggy liked the logging display the best, because it had pictures of the nearby provincial park before all the really big trees were cut down. Josée's favourite was the display of women's clothes, long dresses and parasols, funny old boots and creaky corsets. Alan preferred the section about the old Laingford Jail. There were real handcuffs in a glass case, plus an old leather-covered notebook where some long-ago policeman had written down his case notes.

Alan led the group past all the usual displays to the one at the back of the museum. "It's this one over here," he said. A sign said "The Keewin Inn Era". Two mannequins dressed in formal clothes danced in front of a backdrop that looked like a big porch looking out over a lake. "It doesn't fit in with the pioneer stuff, so I guess that's why they put it at the back," he said. "It's from the 1930s. There was a famous sort of dance hall place back then, on an island over on the other side of Steamboat Lake. They had big bands playing there, and people would come in their fancy boats." There were hundreds of photographs, mostly of people dancing, but of musicians, too. Some of the pictures were close-ups of people who looked like movie stars, signed at the bottom.

"It closed in 1950," Alan read aloud from one of the signs.

"Yeah—that place is a golf course now," Monica said. "My dad goes there."

A small café table was set up beside the dancer mannequins, made to look like they had just got up from a meal to have a waltz. Alan pointed to the place settings. "There, see? Like Mr. Sadler's drinking glasses."

All the plates had "Keewin Inn" written on them, and

the glasses did, too. The silhouette logo on the dinnerware was of two people dancing under a crescent moon.

"Well, these museum glasses are still here, Alain, so I guess Mr. Sadler didn't steal them after all," Josée said.

"Yeah, maybe not from the museum," Alan said to Josée, "but where did he get them? Maybe they were stolen from the golf course."

"Hah," Ziggy said. "Like stealing towels and ashtrays from hotel rooms. My dad is always doing that. I told him to bring me a towel from the Amazon."

"That's not exactly a big crime," Josée said.

"But what if somebody—like Dylan—broke into the golf course and took them, though? And maybe Mr. Sadler was supposed to fence them, but he liked them so much, he kept them instead? Wouldn't that prove he was connected to the break-ins, and maybe connected to the stolen Stradder?"

"What is this fence stuff?" Monica said. Josée explained Alan's term for people who sold stolen goods for robbers.

"Alain's still trying to prove that the violin we heard Mr. Sadler play was the stolen one, but he's just making things up, now," Josée said. "I doubt that some glasses from an old dance hall are going to prove anything."

"Fine," Alan said, annoyed. "Be like that." He turned away, heading towards the Laingford Jail display and the handcuffs.

"Wait, you guys," Ziggy said. "Look at this." He was pointing to one of the framed pictures in the Keewin Inn display. It was a close-up of a group of musicians, dressed in tuxedos and smiling widely at the camera. A drum set beside them had "The Eubie Sadler Seven" painted on it in glittery lettering.

"A dance band," Alan said, reading the caption. "He had a dance band, and they played at the Keewin Inn."

"Maybe he was famous, once," Monica said, reading over his shoulder. "In 1945, anyway. Which one is him?"

"It's hard to tell, but maybe that one," Josée said, pointing. "You know, he looks a bit like Mr. Pratt."

"That explains the fancy drinking glasses he had," Josée said. "They must have given them to him as a thank you or something. And if he was a famous musician, there's no way he'd be a fence for stolen stuff, Alain."

"Okay, okay," Alan said. "You win. The violin we heard him play wasn't the Stradder. But we still need to take that oar back to him, right? Maybe we could ask him to play us something. You know—say we'd seen his picture and act all impressed and everything."

Mrs. Weems called to them from the entrance of the museum. "I'm done here, kids. Let's go." As they headed for the door, Ziggy poked Alan's arm. "If we go back there, I'm staying in the boat," he muttered. "He scares me."

*　　*　　*

It was late afternoon by the time they got back to the Weems's. The sun was still strong, and the water sparkled with a fresh breeze off the lake. Perfect for swimming.

While they were changing into swimsuits in the bedroom they would be sharing in the Weems's guest wing—a huge room like a hotel room, with its own bathroom—Ziggy made an annoyed sound. "I forgot my tooth stuff," he said. Ziggy's teeth were being straightened with braces, and there was a whole routine he had to go through.

"What would happen if you skipped a night?" Alan said.

"The dentist said all my teeth would fall out, but I think he was kidding," Ziggy said. "I'll have to call Vati and ask him to bring it, I guess. Crud. He'll be mad." While Ziggy made the call, Alan walked out to the patio where the girls were waiting. Beside them, the big barbeque gleamed in the sun like a galactic battleship, ready for takeoff.

"That food last night was really good," Alan said, remembering.

"We'll be having the same thing tonight, I guess," Monica said. "Leftovers."

"Pretty good leftovers, if there are any shrimp left," Ziggy said, joining them. "Vati says it's okay to skip tooth-duty for one night. I didn't tell him about the ice cream."

"Well, when you're hungry again, we can just go down to the kitchen and make supper ourselves," said Monica. "Mrs. Holloway, that's our housekeeper, said she'd light the staff barbecue for us. It's a little one, down by where we ate last night."

"I don't know how you can even *think* of food after that sundae you ate, Zig," Josée said. "Let's swim, first, anyway."

"And can I really try out one of those kayaks?" Ziggy said.

"We're allowed to use everything except the motorboats,"

90

Monica said. "There's a paddleboat down there, too. We'll have the whole beach to ourselves."

The beach wasn't empty, though. When they got down to the water, they found Mr. Pratt there, stretched out on a deck chair like an advertisement for suntan lotion. A thick smell of coconut was in the air. He heard them coming and turned, lifting his sunglasses and giving them a brilliant smile. He had a bandage on his forehead, but Alan thought it just made him look like some superhero after a fight. Would he keep the bandage on for the concert? Probably.

"Hi, kids," he called out in a friendly voice. "Don't mind me—I'm just catching some Kuskawa rays before the rehearsal. Just pretend I'm not here."

"As if," Monica said very quietly, and wrapped her towel around herself like she was suddenly cold. She was wearing the green bikini again.

"We're sorry to hear about your accident and the violin getting stolen," Alan said to the musician. "How's your head?"

Mr. Pratt touched his bandage gingerly with the tips of his fingers. "I'm fine, thanks. We violinists are tough. Hey, you're Al, right? Sylvia just told me you offered to lend me your violin. That was nice of you. Thanks." Sylvia? Alan guessed that must be Mrs. Weems. He felt his face getting red.

"I didn't really mean it," he said. But that sounded rude, and Mr. Pratt's friendly smile faltered. "I—I just mean my violin wouldn't be a good stand-in for the Stradivarius," he added in a rush.

91

"It's not the instrument, you know. It's the way you play it," Mr. Pratt said, stiffening.

"Of course. I didn't mean...well, you're going to borrow a good one from someone in the orchestra, anyway, right?"

"Yes, if I need to," he said. "But I have a feeling the Stradder will show up before the concert."

"You know who took it?" Ziggy squawked.

"Oh, I have my suspicions," Mr. Pratt said, looking secretive. "But don't worry. I sure don't suspect any of you, if that's what you're thinking."

"Did you tell the police who you think it is?" Alan asked. Did Mr. Pratt suspect Dylan? Had he even *met* Dylan?

"It's none of your business what I told the police, kid," he said. There was an embarrassed little pause, because nobody could think of anything polite to say after that.

"Last one in gets splashed," Ziggy suddenly shouted. It was what his grandfather always said when he swam with them, even though Vati himself usually ended up getting splashed. Once they were all in, the splashfest would get your blood going, in case the water was cold. They all ripped off their towels, ran yelling down the dock and dove or jumped in. Josée, outrunning Ziggy, performed a beautiful dive off the end of the dock. Ziggy cannonballed, screaming like a freight train, and Alan was right behind him. Monica was last by a mile.

"You guys are nuts," she said, laughing and shaking the water out of her eyes after she came up for air. Ziggy splashed her a little bit, giving her a sideways, ready-for-battle grin with a question in it. She grinned right back and let fly with a practiced firestorm of splashing that made him yell. Then they were all in it, and it was madness for a while. Finally, Ziggy brought his hands up in surrender.

"Okay! Okay! I am defeated. I give up," he shouted. "Monica! Awesome technique."

"Thanks. I have an older brother. I learned early," she said. "Come on, Ziggy. Let's get you a kayak." She and Ziggy swam out to the end of the boathouse dock and hauled themselves up.

"You think that slide will hold me?" Josée said to Alan. A tall waterslide of blue plastic dominated the middle of the shallow area. It looked solid—something for big kids, not small ones.

"It would even hold Mr. Pratt, I bet," Alan said. "It looks like one of those water-park ones. Race you."

After a while, Mr. Pratt called over from his deck chair. They looked and he was standing, the sunlight gleaming on his tanned skin. "Looks like fun," he said. "I'd join you if I could, but duty calls. Can you tell Dylan there's a message for him in the boathouse?"

"Dylan? Monica's brother?" Alan said. Mr. Pratt nodded. "Sure, I guess."

"Thanks," Mr. Pratt said and started to walk back up to the house.

"Were you waiting for him?" Alan called. The musician didn't seem to hear the question and didn't turn around.

"That was weird," Josée said, watching him leave. "Why would he be leaving messages for Dylan? Do they know each other?"

"Monica said at the party that he'd been here before, remember? Maybe they made friends then."

Ziggy and Monica came back, both in kayaks. Everyone had a turn trying them out. Josée said she was hooked and took the longest turns. "It's like being a duck, or a loon," she said. "You're so close to the water, it's like you're sitting in it."

They were having such a good time, they didn't notice the sound of the three jet skis, until they were circling the boathouse dock.

"Hey, that's not the Weem Team," Ziggy said. "It's Dylan, but the other two aren't from his usual gang—not the ones we know from school."

"Just ignore them," Monica said. "They won't drive in this far."

Alan remembered the ducklings they'd seen on the river, staying close to shore, where it was safe.

"We're supposed to tell Dylan there's a message from Mr. Pratt in the boathouse," Josée said.

"Really?" Monica said, her eyebrows raised. "Good luck. What kind of message?"

"We don't know," Alan said. "Anyway, they're ignoring *us*. Whew."

Dylan Weems was big for a fifteen-year-old. His friends were big, too, and they looked much older than he was. They tied up their jet skis at the dock like they were tethering horses and followed Dylan through the side door and into the boathouse.

"If they go in, they'll find whatever message there is, *non?*" Josée said. "We won't have to tell him."

"Maybe they came to check the closet," Monica said. "Maybe they're fences."

"They're too young to be that," Alan said. "I think they're the robber gang. Think about it for a second. If Dylan is breaking into cottages at night, he wouldn't be doing it with the Weem Team—they're all younger than he is."

"We never thought of that, did we?" Josée said.

"Let's get out of the water. We could put the kayaks back now and spy on them," Ziggy said.

"Are you crazy?" Alan said.

"No, that's a good idea," Monica said. "They probably went upstairs, and they won't come down while we're there. We could pretend we're leaving, then hide and listen. We have to put the boats away some time, we might as well do it now."

They entered through the open front of the boathouse, Monica and Josée in the kayaks and the boys swimming. Dylan and his companions were certainly upstairs, because they could hear steps overhead and the pounding beat of heavy rock music.

"They won't hear us at all," Ziggy said as the girls got out. They pulled the lightweight boats up out of the water and dragged them into the corner where the lifejackets were piled.

"Hey, look at this," Alan said. He was looking down at the mooring ring set into the dock where Dylan's jet ski had been tied up the night of the party. A folded-up note had been slipped under the heavy steel ring—the first thing you'd see if you were planning to tie up there.

"Dylan" was written on the outside in thick, black marker.

Eleven

W e have to read it," Ziggy said.

"We can't—it's like, illegal to read somebody else's mail," Alan said.

Ziggy sighed out loud. "TV detectives do it all the time," he said.

"If we're going to read it, we better do it soon," Monica said. They were all standing in a circle, looking down at the folded piece of paper. Nobody had touched it yet. "We'll be dead if Dylan catches us."

"We could just take it," Josée said. "But that's illegal, too, right, *M'seiu le détective?*"

"Oh, all right, we'll read it," Alan said. "But somebody's got to be a lookout."

"I will," Monica said. "If they turn the music off, though, run. It means they're coming down. I'll watch the stairs." She moved over to stand by the door leading to the upstairs apartment. It was open, and the sound of the rock music from above seemed to make the walls shake.

Alan reached down and carefully extracted the note from its resting place under the mooring ring.

"Are you worried about fingerprints?" Josée asked.

Alan glanced up at her to see if she was kidding. It was hard to tell.

"Maybe. It might be evidence," he said.

He opened the note, and they all read it. It was scribbled in pen on a torn-off scrap of paper. One corner of the paper had musical notes on it.

I know who paid you to take it.
Bring it back and I won't tell on you.
    H.P.

"Well, we all know who H.P. is, anyway," Alan said. "I bet there's a corner missing from some of his sheet music."

"Okay, let's put it back quickly, before they come," Ziggy said. Just then, the music stopped. Ziggy and Josée ran, and Alan and Monica were right behind them.

They hid in the bushes and waited for Dylan and his friends to come out.

"He'll know we read it," Alan whispered to the others. "I only shoved it back under the ring-thing. I didn't have time to refold it."

"He may not see it, anyway," Monica said. "His jet ski is tied up outside, remember? So, don't keep me in suspense. What did it say?"

Ziggy did a Mr. Pratt impression. "I know who paid you to take it," he said. "Bring it back and I won't tell on you. H.P."

"Wow," Monica said. "He thinks Dylan stole the violin? Why aren't the police here?"

"We don't think he told them," Alan said. He and

Josée recounted the conversation they had earlier with Mr. Pratt.

"It looks like he's threatening to tell on Dylan unless he gets the violin back," Alan said, thinking out loud. "And he thinks someone paid Dylan to take it. Who would do that?"

"What if it *wasn't* Dylan who took it?" Josée said.

"If he tells the police he suspects Dylan, there's going to be a big mess, no matter what," Monica said. The others looked at each other, remembering what Monica had said about her family breaking up if Dylan was arrested.

"Then *we* have to find the violin first, " Alan said. "And soon."

"Get down!" Monica said suddenly. "They're coming out." They crouched back behind the bushes and watched as Dylan and his big friends emerged from the side door of the boathouse. They seemed to be arguing. Alan strained his ears to hear what they were saying. Dylan followed the other two to where the jet skis were moored. They got on theirs, but Dylan stayed on the dock.

"Tonight!" Dylan almost shouted, as they fired up the engines. He looked really mad. "With or without you guys—tonight!" They roared away. After a moment, Dylan got on his jet ski and drove it slowly around to the open front of the boathouse, disappearing inside.

"He'll see the note now *bien sûr*." Josée said.

"We should go before he comes out again. Let's get some food," Monica said.

* * *

They cooked a big pile of shrimp and hamburgers, fighting over the grill tongs and pretending to be celebrity chefs. Mrs. Holloway, the housekeeper, stayed in the background and didn't say much, except to make sure they cleaned up their own mess. It didn't take them long, with everybody helping. At least, she didn't make them clean the barbecue grill.

"Justin will do it later," Mrs. Holloway said.

"Wow. Dad must've been really mad," Monica said, but Mrs. Holloway just lifted an eyebrow at her. Alan had seen Mrs. Weems do the same eyebrow-thing. It probably meant the same as "you are such a difficult person"—his mother's line.

"Now that we've been refueled," Alan said, "we should go take that oar back to Mr. Sadler before it gets dark."

"I just *knew* you were going to say that," Ziggy said. "I wanted to check out Monica's computer. Josée says it's awesome."

"Yes—come and see Monica's room, first," Josée said. "It's bigger than our living room at home."

It was huge, Alan had to admit when he saw it. She had everything, a TV, a massive computer system, a CD player and her own bathroom. Her bed was all covered in white ruffles, and there were ruffles on the window and around the dresser. Alan though it would be like living in the middle of a wedding cake.

"It's very white," he said.

"Yeah, I once dropped a full Coke in here, and Mother had a fit," Monica said. "The white was her idea, not mine. She says I can do what I want with it after I turn thirteen."

"What would you change?" Josée said, flopping down on the bed, which sort of billowed up around her, like marshmallow frosting.

"Everything," Monica said.

"Can I try your computer?" Ziggy said.

"Go ahead," she said, joining Josée on the bed. "There's tons of games on there, if you want. I use it for homework, mostly. Hey, Josée, I got some new ballet stuff last week, you want to see?"

Ziggy and Alan logged on.

"Why don't we look up Mr. Pratt?" Alan said. "Google him and see if he has a website." Ziggy typed the musician's name into a search engine and waited. Lots of sites popped up, among them www.hughpratt.com, and he clicked on it. There were lots of pictures, a biography, some reviews of his CDs, and a link to "more pictures."

"Pretty boring," Ziggy said after a minute. "It's all like a big commercial for Mr. Pratt."

"Go back to the search list," Alan said. This time they clicked on a site that contained a magazine article about the Stradivarius contest. It had a list of all the violin players who competed for the use of the famous violin, with pictures of each one.

"Hey, stop a minute. Scroll up," Alan said suddenly. Then he pointed to the screen. "That's the violin player from the orchestra—Annette—the one who had the fight with Mr. Pratt at the party, remember?" Monica and Josée came over to look.

"That's her all right," Josée said. "So she was in the competition, too."

"Yeah, remember she said he flirted with the girls, and that was how he won the contest?" Ziggy said. "What did she mean?"

"I know what kind of flirting he does," Monica said in a hard voice. They turned to look at her. "He treats you really nice when you can do something for him, then he suddenly calls you a little pest and tells you to buzz off."

"Ew. *Quel* creep," Josée said.

"Is that why you said that it must, you know, suck to be Candace, my sister?" Alan said. "You thought he was acting like her boyfriend?"

"More like her king," Monica said. "Last time he was here, I ran around carrying things for him just like she was, and he was so sweet to me. Then all of a sudden it was like I was just something on the bottom of his shoe."

"When was this?" Alan asked.

"Two years ago, before he got really famous. He came up to do a solo recital, and my parents had an afternoon barbecue."

They turned back to the screen. "So if this Annette and Mr. Pratt were in the same contest," Ziggy said, "maybe he treated *her* like that, too. Maybe she paid Dylan to steal the violin to get back at him."

"But she wouldn't let him boss her around in the first place, would she?" Josée said.

"Probably not," Alan said. "She made it sound like maybe he flirted with somebody else, and that helped him win the contest."

"How would that make him win a violin contest?" Ziggy asked, still scrolling down the pictures. "Look, there's the judges. Three of them. Anyone recognize them?"

Nobody did, and they watched as more pictures came up on the screen, many obviously taken during a party like the one at the Weems's house the night before.

"There's Mr. Pratt," Josée said, pointing. "And look—he's got his arm around some girl." The caption read: *Contestant Hugh Pratt shares a joke with young fan Selena Ryerson at the opening reception.*

"Go back up to the judges' pictures, Zig," Alan said. "There. Look. Conrad Ryerson. He was one of the judges."

"And if Selena Ryerson was his daughter, and she was a fan, and he was really nice to her…" Ziggy said.

"Then maybe he voted for Mr. Pratt to win," Josée finished. *"Étonnant!"*

"And that's why Annette said he didn't win fairly," Alan said.

"So maybe Mr. Pratt is right. Maybe she *did* pay Dylan to steal the violin, to get back at him," Monica said.

"Yeah, and look, here's a picture of the top three winners," Ziggy said. "It says the second and third prize was money. But Mr. Pratt got the violin. And look who's in second place." It was Annette.

The evening was approaching, and the sun was beginning to set. Alan looked out at the lake through Monica's white-ruffled curtains, then turned to Ziggy, who was still surfing the internet.

"Zig, can I borrow your canoe?" he said.

"You're still planning to go over to the island?" Monica said.

"I want to get that oar back to Mr. Sadler," he said.

102

"And I want to make sure in my own mind that he doesn't have the Stradder. It's been bugging me."

"Even though we've practically proved that Dylan stole it for Mr. Pratt's enemy, Annette?" Ziggy said.

"We haven't proved anything," Alan said. "We just know that she might possibly have a motive. No TV detective would stop there."

"He won't like you dropping in on him," Ziggy said. "Remember he said he didn't like visitors."

"Yeah, but we'd be bringing back his oar."

"We don't even know it's his," Josée said. "But I'll go with you, if you want. I'm not scared."

"Who said I was scared?" Ziggy said. "I'm in."

"Is there room for four of us?" Monica said.

Alan looked out the window again. "The lake's really calm now," he said. "There's no wind any more, so we should be okay. We'll take a couple of flashlights, though, in case it gets dark before we get back."

"*If* we get back," Ziggy said, darkly.

Twelve

"Your mother would absolutely kill us if she knew we were doing this," Ziggy said to Alan a little later, when they were putting on lifejackets at the boathouse. There was no sign of Dylan, and the lights in the upstairs apartment were out.

"Well, hopefully, she won't know," Alan said. Secretly, he wondered if they were doing a really stupid thing, but Josée's remark about being scared had made them all want to prove that they weren't.

It would stay light out until about nine o'clock, so they had roughly an hour to paddle over to Eubie Sadler's island, return the oar and get back before nightfall. The lake was as still as a glass mirror, and it was very quiet.

"Do you hear what I hear?" Alan said to the others a little later, turning from his place in the bow of the canoe. They had crossed over to the island with no trouble at all and were very close to Mr. Sadler's wharf. Through the trees, they could see a softly glowing light, and from the same direction came violin music, very soft and sweet.

"It could be a recording," Josée said. They had tied the oar to a rope at the back of the canoe and towed it over.

104

It had followed behind them like a large, stiff water-snake. Ziggy untied it and handed it up to Alan, who had climbed out and onto the wharf. "You know, we could just put the oar into his boat and go," Ziggy said.

"You can stay down here if you want," Alan said. "I have to find out if he's got the Stradder." He put the oar quietly into the rowboat. It looked exactly like the other one, Alan thought, but then all oars looked alike to him, anyway.

"Someone should stay down here and guard the canoe," Monica said. "Me and Ziggy will."

Alan and Josée exchanged a look. "Okay," Josée said. "We'll be quick."

"We won't have to knock on the door or anything," Alan whispered, as they made their way up the path. They were both trying to walk without making any noise. "We can just peek in and look."

"How will you know just by looking that it's the Stradder?" Josée said.

"I'll just know, Josée," he said. Before they got to the top of the stairs leading up to the cabin, they both left the staircase and took to the bushes, in case Mr. Sadler heard them and came out to investigate. It was getting dark rapidly now, and the bushes were thick, but they made almost no sound until Alan tripped over something.

"Shhh!" Josée said, grabbing his arm. "He'll hear us." Alan was looking at what he'd tripped over. It was a violin case, open and empty.

"Mon dieu, is that the Stradder case?" Josée said.

"I don't think so," Alan said. "The one we carried in

from the van was really expensive—leather, and sort of brown. This one's black and beat-up."

"But no violin," Josée said. "Did Mr. Sadler just throw it away? What's it doing in the bushes?"

"I don't think he threw it here," Alan said, after a moment. "But someone did." He picked it up. "If Mr. Sadler hears us and comes out, we can say we brought back the oar and we found this. I think I know what happened, though."

"What?"

"Shhh. I'll explain later." Together they tiptoed up to the cabin and found a low window around the side where they could peer in without being seen. The music was still playing, very softly.

In the living room of the cabin, Eubie Sadler stood with a violin tucked under his chin, playing with his eyes closed and a dreamy smile on his face. Alan recognized the music. it was a piece he'd played himself, a simple folk tune in a minor key that sounded like crying. He imagined Mr. Sadler in a dance band at the old Keewin Inn, playing in front of an old-fashioned microphone while glittery couples swirled around a polished floor. Maybe Mr. Sadler was imagining the same thing. The room looked okay now. The old man had cleaned up the mess the robbers had left, and it looked like he had painted over the bad words that had been scrawled on the walls. Next to him on a chair was a brown leather violin case.

"It's the Stradder, I know it," Alan whispered. Josée nodded. She believed him now. But what on earth were they going to do about it?

"Let's go," Josée whispered. "We can't go in and accuse him. And the others are waiting. We can phone the police from Monica's house."

Alan didn't want to phone the police at all. Watching Mr. Sadler play, wrapped in his memories, made a lump rise in his throat. And he *did* think he knew what had happened. He told the others when they got back down to the canoe.

"Remember the drowned violin?" he said. "The one we found yesterday near where you found the oar today, Monica? I think it was Mr. Sadler's. And this," he displayed the battered violin case they'd found in the bushes, "is his case."

"Why would he throw away his violin?" Monica asked.

"He didn't. The people who broke into his cabin did," Alan said.

"Dylan and his thugs," Ziggy said. "So—what? They stole Mr. Sadler's violin and drowned it, then stole the Stradder and gave it to Mr. Sadler to say sorry or something?"

"I don't know," Alan said. "But we know he's got the Stradder now, no matter what."

"We can call the police when we get back," Josée said again. "It'll take the suspicion off Dylan, and then everything will be fine for Monica."

"Everything won't be fine for Mr. Sadler," Alan said.

"But you'll get a medal for being a hero detective," Ziggy said. "You'll probably get your picture in the paper and everything."

"I think we should wait," Alan said. They had got back in the canoe and were heading back to Monica's place. It was dark enough now that Monica, in the middle and not paddling, was holding the two flashlights pointing forwards and backwards to act as lights, in case they met any motorboats.

"Wait for what? Mr. Pratt needs the Stradder back for the concert," Josée said. "And if he doesn't get it back, he'll tell the police Dylan took it."

"I have an idea to get it back, and nobody will ever know," Alan said. But he wouldn't say anything more. And when they got back to the boathouse, Dylan was standing on the dock waiting for them.

*   *   *

"Where have you been?" he asked belligerently, when they got close enough. "Mrs. Holloway's looking for you. You're in big trouble, Monica."

"Not as big as you're in," she said. Dylan had his arms crossed. He was frowning.

"These are your little friends, are they? Well, you're all in trouble. You know you're not allowed to go out in a boat at night."

They quickly beached the canoe and clambered up onto the dock to take their lifejackets off.

"We just went for a paddle to watch the sunset. We're not in trouble, Dylan. Not like the kind of trouble you're in." Alan was amazed that Monica was standing up to him. He had seen Dylan at work playing the bully a dozen times with his gang, the Weem Team. It was good to see someone talking back to him, but it was scary, too.

Dylan was known to get pushy.

"What do you mean by that, little sister?" he asked, taking a threatening step towards her.

"I mean that we know about the stuff in that closet upstairs, big brother. And we know where it came from." She was a lot shorter than he was, but she wasn't backing down. Everybody held their breath.

"Oh, so it was you snooping in there the other night, was it? I should have known. Now listen, all of you. That stuff is none of your business, and if you don't want to get hurt, you'll forget all about it, okay?" Dylan's words were tough, but Alan thought he looked scared suddenly.

"You don't scare us, Dylan," Monica said.

"Well, you should be scared," he said. "This isn't kid stuff, you know."

"*You're* a kid," Ziggy piped up.

Dylan sneered at him. "You want to find out what kind of kid I am, buddy? Come here and I'll show you." His fists were clenched, and he looked like he wanted to throw Ziggy in the water.

"No thanks," Ziggy said. "I'm just saying you're not much older than us."

"Dylan," Monica said, her voice soft, now. "Look, nobody cares where that stuff in the closet came from, really. But you have to get rid of it before the police find it. You could go to jail."

"I had nothing to do with it," Dylan said, quickly. "I was just storing it for a friend, that's all."

"Those friends who were here today? Not your usual friends," she said.

"I have lots of friends you don't know about, little sister," he said. Alan thought it sounded more like he didn't have many real friends at all.

"Fine," Monica said. "Whatever. But what are you going to say if the police come looking for that violin down here and find your little stash of stolen goods? You think they're going to believe that you were just storing it for a friend? Get real, Dylan."

"What violin?" he said, sharply. "The Strad? I didn't touch it—swear to God."

"Tell that to the police," Alan said.

"What do you little kids know about all this?" he said, his eyes narrowing. "You haven't gone squealing to the cops, have you? If you have, you'll regret it, big time."

"We haven't said anything," Monica said. "Dylan, you know what'll happen if you get into trouble again, don't you? Dad will send you to that boot camp place, and Mother will bail on us for sure. How could you do this to us?" She was getting a little teary, Alan thought.

"They don't need to know anything about it," Dylan said. He sounded as if he knew what Monica was talking about—like whatever doom Monica had predicted was something that both Weems kids knew was true.

"What if Mr. Pratt tells on you?" Alan said. Dylan glared at him.

"How did you—? Oh, I get it. You snooped into that note he left, didn't you? Jeez, you kids are a pain. Well, listen. That big creep thinks he knows something, but he doesn't. I didn't touch his stupid violin."

"But if he tells the police you did, it'll be the same

thing," Monica said. "When they find your hidden stuff, I mean. They'll know you're a robber, and you'll be arrested."

"They're not *going* to find it," Dylan said. "It'll be gone by tomorrow morning. And then the police can snoop around all they want, they won't be able to pin a thing on me."

"You'd better hope so," Monica said.

"So can I rely on you kids not to say anything?" he said, in a suddenly softer tone.

"Maybe if you leave us alone from now on when we're in the canoe," Alan said.

"Oh, that. Heck, we were just fooling around. Can't you take a joke?"

"That was no joke," Ziggy said. "We could have drowned."

"You're too young to be out in a canoe by yourselves, anyway," Dylan said. All four of them just stood there, their hands on their hips, not saying anything. They had him cornered.

"Okay, then it's a deal," Dylan said, finally. "I'll leave you guys alone, and you keep your mouths shut about the stuff upstairs. But I swear, if I find out you've squealed, I'll make sure you wish you'd never been born." He turned away and stomped into the boathouse.

"Whew," Alan said when he'd gone. "I never thought I'd have that long of a conversation with Dylan Weems without getting creamed."

"He's such an idiot," Monica said.

"You said he's been in trouble before?" Josée said.

"Yes—he can't seem to stay out of it. And Dad gets mad and threatens to send him to some military school place, and they fight about it. After a while, they make up and Dad gives Dylan some new toy to keep him happy, like the jet ski. Mother says Dylan's spoiled and out of control, and they argue about him all the time. That's why I think this mess will be the last straw. Dad won't be able to ignore it this time."

"So you think his friends will come back tonight and take that stuff away?" Ziggy said.

"Well, he practically said so, didn't he? He'd better hope it's gone before Mr. Pratt tells the police he stole the violin, and they come to get him."

"But Dylan didn't steal the violin—Mr. Sadler did," Josée said.

"We don't know that Mr. Sadler *stole* it," Alan said. "We just know he has it. And if we can get it back before Mr. Pratt tells on Dylan, then maybe there won't be a 'last straw' at all, Monica."

"And how in the world are we going to do that?" Monica asked.

"Don't worry," Alan said. "I have a plan."

Thirteen

Before bed, Monica suggested that they all get together after midnight to keep watch on Dylan.

"He knows that the rehearsal for the concert is tonight, and our parents and Mr. Pratt won't get back until really late," Monica said. "I think he'll wait until they're asleep before he moves the stolen stuff."

"Won't he do it before they get back, after he knows we're in bed?" Alan said.

"Not while Justin and Mrs. Holloway are still up," Monica said. The housekeeper and the beefy security man were playing cards in the staff lounge. "They won't go to bed until my parents get back, and the lounge window looks right out at the lake. Dylan won't risk it."

"You'd think the sound of the jet skis out on the lake would wake everybody up, at that time of night," Alan said.

"Maybe they'll take the stuff away by car," Ziggy said.

"Well, no matter how they do it, I want to be sure it happens," Monica said. "Mr. Pratt could tell on Dylan at any moment. He might have done it already."

"I doubt it," Alan said. "He's a serious musician, and he's rehearsing tonight. He won't be thinking about anything but the music. Especially if he's rehearsing on a second-rate violin."

"So what time should we set your alarm for?" Josée asked Monica.

"Let's say one a.m.," Monica said. "If the grown-ups don't wake us first. They'll probably have a nightcap before they go to bed."

"What's a nightcap?"

"The stuff in the cut-glass bottle on the bar, usually. I think it's brandy. They have it in big balloony glasses."

"We don't have an alarm," Alan said.

"We'll come and get you," Monica said. "There's back stairs we can use, but I'll have to show you the way."

Alan and Ziggy had no way of knowing if the adults' return woke the girls up, but they were both wide awake the moment they heard the car doors slam outside their window. They heard soft voices and footfalls on the gravel path, then the sound of the heavy front door closing. "Now we have to stay awake until they're in bed," Alan said.

"I'll have to get up, then," Ziggy said, putting his feet on the floor. "I'll just go to sleep again, otherwise."

"Me, too." They put on their shoes and waited. Both boys had gone to sleep in their clothes.

From downstairs, they could hear the clink of glasses. "That's the nightcap," Ziggy whispered. Then very softly came the sound of music.

"Opera," Alan said. "Monica said her dad listens to it all the time."

"Do you like opera music?"

"Not unless it's in English," Alan said, "and it usually

114

isn't. Mom took us to see *Die Fledermaus* in the city once, and I fell asleep."

"*Fledermaus* means bat," Ziggy said.

"Yeah. I thought it would be like an opera version of *Batman*," Alan said. "It wasn't."

They heard footsteps in the hallway outside their door, and both of them instinctively jumped back into bed, shoes and all, in case someone was coming to check that they were asleep. The footsteps continued down the hall, then they heard the sound of a key in a lock and a door opening.

"Mr. Pratt's room must be next to ours," Alan whispered. "I hope he's a sound sleeper." There was no need to guess about when the musician fell asleep at least. In less than ten minutes, the sound of heavy snoring came echoing through the walls.

"Well, we didn't need to worry about not having an alarm clock," Ziggy muttered. "He's louder than a recess bell."

Not long after that, there was a soft knock on the bedroom door, and Monica and Josée tiptoed in, stifling giggles.

"Sorry about your luck," Monica said. "I didn't know he snored."

"Maybe he'll choke in his sleep," Ziggy said, optimistically.

They crept back along the wood-floored hallway to a set of stairs, hidden around a corner at the far end.

"We have to be really quiet, because Justin and Mrs. Holloway sleep down there. They have to get up early, though, so they'll be fast asleep by now," Monica whispered.

"What about your parents?" Alan said.

Monica pointed toward the main staircase leading down into the living room. "That's why we're not going that way," she said. "Their suite is beside the living room, and sometimes they stay up arguing. If they *are* still up, they won't hear us, as long as we keep to the back of the house."

Creeping along the hallway, Alan tried to do Ziggy's sneaking-in-the-woods trick, the one his friend had taught him last summer. You were supposed to walk using your whole foot, heel to toe, instead of tip-toeing. With his knees slightly flexed, alert for twigs and dry leaves, Ziggy could move along as quietly as a ghost in the forest. His Vati had taught him. It was a useful skill for a detective to have, Alan thought, and he liked to practice sometimes. Now, he was using it for real.

He was amazed at how quiet four kids could be when they were working at it. Monica hit a creaking floorboard and turned around to make sure the others knew to avoid it. It was like a very serious game of Follow-the-Leader.

Just before they got to the staff kitchen doorway, they all heard the sound of a fridge door opening. It was like thunder in the silence. They all froze. The hallway was dark, except for the little dim floorlights that were everywhere, like tiny nightlights. A stream of bluish light poured from the kitchen doorway. Someone was getting a midnight snack. Monica turned to the others with her finger to her lips. Then she tiptoed forward and slipped her head around the door very quickly, then back.

"It-th Juthtin," she whispered. Alan wondered why she was lisping, until he tried it himself, later. When you're whispering, anything with an "s" sound makes a noise. A lisp doesn't.

They backed up along the hallway and slipped through the open door of a small storage room. Monica closed the door slowly, leaving a crack to peek through. Suddenly she held up a hand to say "keep still, don't move," and they felt, rather than heard, someone walk back down the hall. Moments later, they heard another door open and close.

Monica beckoned, and they all followed again, this time all the way to the end of the hall, quietly out the door and into the night.

Quickly, they moved away from the house and gathered in the shadows beside a cedar hedge.

"Whew, *mon coeur,*" Josée said, her hand on her chest. "That was close."

It was beautiful out. The air was warm and perfumed by the big flowerbeds framing the lawn. The grass was dewy, and there was a big moon, not quite full. A gentle breeze came in from the lake, which seemed to dance in the light. They still whispered, but Alan felt like shouting with the delicious sense of adventure that was creeping over him.

"How did you know to do the lisping thing?" he asked Monica.

"Yeah, that was cool," Ziggy said.

"I go to private school," Monica said. "You learn how to be quiet pretty quickly when your teachers sleep next door."

"Ew," Josée said.

"Sans blague," said Monica.

They were all dressed in jeans and dark, long-sleeved T-shirts. Alan had suggested this earlier, so that they would be more invisible. Ziggy had wanted to black their faces as well but was overruled. They made their way slowly and quietly down to the boathouse and hid in the bushes by the back stairs, their escape route of the day before.

"They won't use the main door on the other side," Monica said. "You can see that from the house." They did not have long to wait. In the distance, they heard the low, glugging sound of an inboard motor. At the same time, a dim light appeared in the boathouse apartment.

The engine sound came closer, and soon a small cruising boat pulled quietly up to the narrow dock at the bottom of the stairs. There were two figures in it, Dylan's friends from earlier, the ones he had yelled at. They were both dressed in black, and Alan thought privately that they looked even bigger at night than they had during the day. He had a feeling that Dylan's friends wouldn't be quite as open to negotiation as Dylan had been.

The teenagers met on the stairs. Dylan had come out carrying a box as soon as they moored the boat. There was a whispered exchange (they didn't use the lisping-trick, so Alan could hear them, sort of hissing like snakes), then they got to work.

Unloading the hidden things from the closet took time. There seemed to be a lot of it.

"It mutht be a big clothet," Josée whispered.

Finally, they were finished, and covered the mound of goods with a blanket Dylan had brought down. Then he climbed into the boat with his friends, and off they went, the low growl of the inboard engine fading quickly as the boat headed out into open water.

They crept out of hiding and watched until it disappeared around the point. "Maybe they're headed for town," Ziggy said. "They'd better hope they don't meet the marine patrol, eh?"

"Well, that's a relief," Monica said. "At least the stuff is out of here. Now if Mr. Pratt talks to the police, and they come and search, they won't find anything."

"I'd love to follow them," Alan said.

"Are you crazy?" Ziggy said. "Do you have a death-wish?"

"I'm just saying," Alan said. "If I was older and had a boat, I would."

"We could go in the canoe," Josée said.

"We'd never catch up to them," Monica said. "Anyway, I don't care where they go. They're gone, that's the main thing."

*   *   *

They all made it back to the house without meeting anyone. Nobody seemed to have heard the boat engine, and all was quiet and dark inside. They parted on the back stairs and promised each other they would try to get up early.

"I may not sleep, anyway," Josée said. "I'm wide awake."

When they got back to their room, Ziggy said the same thing, and so did Alan. But it wasn't excitement that would keep them awake. Mr. Pratt, in his room just down the hall, was still snoring like a moose.

Fourteen

The next morning, Mrs. Nearing came to get them in the van, so they could go along and help set up for the concert. Alan was used to this. "I'm usually volunteered by my mom to be the gopher, and set up chairs and stuff at the auditorium," he explained to Monica. Ziggy and Josée had helped once before, too.

"I'd love to come, but I'm supposed to help Mother get ready for the reception," Monica said. There would be another party at the Weems' home that night. Mrs. Weems had told Alan's mother that the kids could all stay over again, if they wished. "They can keep each other company, and you'll be able to let down your hair a bit, Mary-Anne," Mrs. Weems said, and Mrs. Nearing had agreed on one condition.

"Mr. Ziegler called and said he had a lesson slot free before lunch," she said to Alan. "I told him you'd be there."

"Awww, Mo-om," Alan said.

"No lesson, no overnight." It was a simple as that.

Both Ziggy and Josée said they would get permission from home. Ziggy had to pick up his braces stuff ("I can't miss another night, or my teeth *will* fall out," he said), and Josée wanted to choose an outfit for the concert. They would all be going together, and Mrs. Weems made it clear that jeans and T-shirts were not allowed.

*   *   *

The Laingford Auditorium was a big, open space like a gym, with a stage at one end. Hundreds of folding chairs were kept on rolling racks under the stage, and Alan and his friends were assigned to set them up.

"Four hundred chairs," Alan announced to his friends, after being given instructions by a woman in floaty clothes, holding a clip board. "This could take awhile." They set to it, and worked hard for an hour, while men and women with ladders moved back and forth, setting up the stage lights.

"I love the feel of a performance space before a show," the clipboard woman said, coming to say thanks while they were taking a much-needed water break. "It's all so exciting! Oh, excuse me. Mr. Pratt has just arrived. I guess he wants to check that everything's okay." She fluttered away towards the entrance, where Mr. Pratt stood, surveying the scene with his arms crossed.

"Mamère would call him a control freak," Josée said.

They went back to work. Near the end they were all sweaty from heaving the chairs around. "They aren't that heavy to start with," Ziggy said at one point, "but after a row or two, they weigh a ton."

"Good workout for paddling, Zig," Alan said. But Ziggy was right. His own arms were starting to ache. "I'm just going to the washroom. Be back in a sec." He really did have to pee, but more importantly, he had just caught a glimpse of somebody moving down the side-aisle and slipping into the backstage area, where Mr. Pratt had gone. He was certain that it was Annette. He followed. Maybe he could listen in. A detective wouldn't call it eavesdropping, he was sure. It was surveillance.

The hall had three dressing rooms, two big ones for men and women and one smaller, luxury model used for guest artists. The local amateur theatre group used the hall every year, and Alan had once been in the children's chorus of a musical, so he knew the backstage well. He ducked into the men's dressing room, moments after Annette had entered the one next door, the guest artist one. To Alan's right was a long countertop and mirrors with lights, enough room for a dozen actors. Above the bank of mirrors was an air vent. The vent was like a loudspeaker, amplifying the conversation from the next room perfectly. He held his breath and listened.

"…don't know why you think you can just summon me and I'll appear," Annette was saying.

"You did, though, didn't you?" came Mr. Pratt's smooth drawl.

"What did you want to tell me that you couldn't say over the phone, Hugh?" she said.

"You know perfectly well."

"No, I don't."

"Look, Annette, let's not fool around. I know you paid that Weems kid to take the Stradder and give me a scare, okay? Point taken. But the joke's over, and I want it back. Before tonight."

"I don't have the faintest idea what you're talking about," Annette said.

"Do I have to spell it out for you? I saw you talking to the kid at the party the other night, first of all."

"He was talking to the oboe player, Steve, actually," Annette said. "They were talking about motorcycles. Steve gave me a ride over there on his Harley."

"I'm not saying Steve wasn't in on it, too," Mr. Pratt said.

"In on what? You think I arranged for Giles Weems's son to steal your stupid violin? You're out of your mind."

"I saw him," Mr. Pratt said.

Alan almost gasped aloud. Then Dylan *had* stolen it, after all?

"You saw him take it?"

"Not exactly. It was late, and I couldn't sleep. So I took the Stradder out to the patio with me to play a little in the moonlight," he said.

"Serenading yourself? That's soooo cute," she said. From her tone of voice, Alan couldn't tell if she was being sarcastic or not.

"Yeah, well. You know, I'd play it every minute of the day, if I could. Annette—I know we haven't been all that friendly since the competition, and I know what you think of me…"

"I'm sorry I said what I said at the party, Hugh. I was kind of out of it."

"No kidding. But listen, I said I saw him. The kid, I mean. I played a little, then I laid down on one of those stone benches to look up at the stars, and I heard a noise and there he was, coming up the patio stairs. I tried to sit up, but I sort of slipped and fell off the bench. I must have whacked my head on the way down. I was out like a light."

"Ouch," she said.

"And when I woke up a couple of hours later, with one hell of a headache, the Stradder was gone—case and all."

"Why didn't you tell the police?" she asked. "Why pretend somebody had beaned you?"

"I wasn't thinking straight. I just immediately put two and two together and figured it was a prank."

"And you thought I was the prankster? Thanks a lot."

"Swear to me it wasn't you," he said.

"I'm not swearing anything, Hugh," she said. "But listen, if the Weems boy was there just before you knocked yourself out, how come he didn't call for help? He wouldn't have left you there."

"Maybe stealing the Stradder distracted him," he said.

"He seemed like a nice enough kid to me," Annette said. "Maybe he didn't see you at all—just walked on by. It was the middle of the night, right?"

"Then who stole my violin?" Mr. Pratt said.

"How should I know? Listen, Hugh. I appreciate you keeping quiet about your suspicions until now. I'm not interested in being interviewed by the police again. They talked to me already. I guess somebody reported that little scene we had at the party."

"It wasn't me," he said.

"It doesn't matter. I didn't tell them anything, anyway. Just that I'd had too much to drink, which was true. But

I think you should tell the police what really happened. It wasn't a prank—at least if it was, it didn't come from me. And the violin's still missing, right?"

"Oh, God. That means somebody really *did* steal it. Professionals. My career will be ruined. I'm doomed."

"It's always about you, isn't it Hugh?" Annette said. "Maybe they should have awarded the Stradivarius to somebody who could take care of it." There was silence for a moment. Alan wondered if Mr. Pratt was crying. It sounded like he might be, hard as it was to imagine.

"Anyway, for your sake, I hope whoever took it *does* bring it back. And break a leg tonight, eh? It was really nice of Fiona to lend you her instrument. I hope you appreciate her sacrifice." Again, no answer from Mr. Pratt. Alan heard the dressing room door slam, and footsteps echoing away. Alan decided to find another washroom, somewhere in the lobby. He didn't want Mr. Pratt to find him back there. And anyway, he had to report back to the others. Time was running out.

*   *   *

"So that's how Mr. Pratt ended up knocked out on the patio," Josée said. "There was no thug at all."

"But the violin was still stolen," Alan said.

"I don't think Dylan could have taken it," Josée said. "He wouldn't have just left Mr. Pratt lying there. Monica's brother may be a creep, but he's not that bad."

"But how did Mr. Sadler get hold of it, then?" Ziggy said.

"We'll find out this afternoon, won't we?" Alan said. "Now there's even more reason to get it back from him as soon as possible. If Mr. Pratt tells the police what really happened, Dylan's in huge trouble."

"Should we tell Monica?" Josée said.

"Maybe not," Alan said after a moment's thought. "At least not yet. She's worried enough already."

Mrs. Nearing had agreed to chauffeur the three of them back to the Weems place after Alan's violin lesson. She was pleased with how quickly they had set up the chairs in the auditorium and had even promised ice cream cones on the way there.

"Come over about noon, you two," she said to Ziggy and Josée, before dropping them off. Alan wasn't sure his mom would be in such a great mood after the lesson— not if Mr. Ziegler flipped out at him the way he expected. But there was nothing he could do about it. Like Mr. Pratt, he felt doomed.

Fifteen

Alan waited outside the door of Mr. Ziegler's studio, feeling like he was at the dentist's. The music teacher gave lessons in his home, a big brick house hear the lookout, overlooking the river. He had a lot of students, and the lessons were tightly booked, so if you got there early, you had to wait in the hall. There was a comfortable bench and some music magazines, but Alan didn't feel like reading. He felt like running.

Inside, someone was playing a complicated piece on the cello. They were really, really good. After the music finished, he heard Mr. Ziegler's voice—a low purr, like a big, expensive car. He sounded pleased, Alan thought, even though he couldn't hear the actual words.

The cello student came out moments later, a tiny kid who couldn't have been more than seven. The instrument case was almost as big as he was.

"Good work, Mr. Johnson," Mr. Ziegler said. "We'll see you next week, yes?" The miniature Mr. Johnson squeaked a goodbye and wrestled his cello down the stairs. It was part of the music teacher's style to call all his students Mister or Ms. It was kind of formal, but Alan liked it. It meant he took you seriously.

"Ah, Mr. Nearing. I'm glad we were able to rebook you," Mr. Ziegler said. "One of my viola students is sick." Alan followed his teacher into the studio. It was a big, bright room with a large window looking out over the water. There was a small piano, a few music stands and performance chairs, and the rest of the space was bare, except for a couple of wooden filing cabinets full of sheet music. The only decoration was a huge painting of a violinist, all swirling colours and movement, as if the musician might jump right out of the frame at any moment. When Alan was younger, he had loved coming here; it was like going to church. It smelled spicy and polished, and the music he made on his violin always sounded much better here than it did anywhere else.

"I thought I'd better tell you right at the beginning that I haven't practiced," Alan said. He had been planning to fake it, but hearing little Mr. Johnson had made him change his mind.

"I see," the music teacher said. "Well, thank you for being honest about it, anyway."

"I'm sorry. I guess I've been really busy," he said, beginning to open his case.

"Leave that for a moment. Let's sit down, okay?" Mr. Ziegler said. Uh-oh. Alan sat.

"Tell me, Mr. Nearing, when was the last time you played the violin—not including our last lesson—umm…two weeks ago, was it?" Alan nodded. He hadn't practiced for that one, either. Mr. Ziegler hadn't said anything, but Alan hadn't exactly been Johnson-perfect that time, either.

"I guess…not for a while," Alan mumbled.

"I hate to bring this up, but can you tell me now often Candace practices?" Mr. Ziegler said.

"No fair—she's like, obsessed," Alan said. "She'd play all day if she was allowed, only Mom makes her go outside so she has a life."

"So you would say that perhaps you don't share your sister's dedication to the instrument?" Mr. Ziegler said, dryly. Alan just shook his head.

"You've been playing for how long?"

"Since I was four," Alan said. "Remember I started on that little violin? Candace taught me to begin with, and then I started coming here."

"So—seven years. That's a long time. A lot of lessons."

"Uh-huh. And I really…*used* to like it, Mr. Ziegler," Alan said. The music teacher nodded and smiled in an easygoing way that made Alan relax a bit.

"People change a lot in seven years," Mr. Ziegler said. "Especially young people. But you know, Mr. Nearing, I am not a cheap teacher. Your mother pays me quite a lot of money for your lessons. You know that, don't you?" Alan nodded again. Actually, he didn't have any idea how much the lessons cost, but Mr. Ziegler's house was pretty nice, if that was any clue.

"So, if your heart's not in playing the violin, are you perhaps interested in something else?"

"I doubt I could take up the cello this late," Alan said. "Not with the head start that other little guy has." They grinned at each other.

"I didn't mean music," Mr. Ziegler said. "You have

129

other interests, perhaps? New friends? Girls, maybe?"

"Not girls," Alan said quickly, blushing. "Not yet, anyway."

"I'm glad to hear it," the music teacher said. "You're a little young to be sacrificing music for love. So—what else?"

"You really want to know?"

"Yes, if you're comfortable telling me. Sports, maybe? Lacrosse?"

"Detection," Alan said. And, once he got started, he told Mr. Ziegler all the rest. But first, he swore the music teacher to secrecy. Mr. Ziegler was the kind of adult who would keep his word, he was sure of it.

"Cross my heart," Mr. Ziegler promised. Alan told his violin teacher all about Mr. Pratt and the Stradivarius— how he'd played the instrument the night of the party, how it had disappeared, and how Alan had found out where it was. He didn't mention Dylan and the stolen goods in the boathouse, and he didn't mention Eubie Sadler by name, although Mr. Ziegler seemed to know right away who he was talking about.

"He was a magnificent musician, years ago," Mr. Ziegler said. "I've met him on occasion. He doesn't strike me as a thieving type, though."

"Well, that's where the Stradder is," Alan said. "And I have a plan to get it back, but I guess I sort of need your help."

"You're playing with fire, Mr. Nearing," he said. "But if I can, without compromising myself, I will."

"All I need you to do is not tell my mom that I want to quit violin. Not yet," Alan said. This was the first time he'd said it aloud, although the conversation had been heading that way. Mr. Ziegler had made it easy for him. Maybe he had students quitting all the time. Alan would bet he had a waiting list, so it wasn't as if he needed the business.

"You would have had to tell her yourself, first, anyway," Mr. Ziegler said. "That's not something I'd do without your permission."

"Thanks," Alan said. "I will tell her—I promise. After tonight. Are you going to the concert?"

"I wouldn't miss it for anything. Hugh Pratt is spectacular, and I haven't heard a Stradivarius played live for years."

"Well, tonight, he'll be playing one," Alan said.

"Good luck, Mr. Nearing," Mr. Ziegler said. "It's been a pleasure knowing you, even if you haven't exactly been my most enthusiastic pupil."

"Thanks, sir," Alan said. "It's been good knowing you, too. And maybe now Mom can pay for twice as many lessons for the person in the family who really has a future."

They shook hands, and Alan picked up his violin case and said goodbye. He hadn't even opened it.

*   *   *

"How was your lesson?" his mom asked, as she usually did, the moment he got home.

"Fine," he said. His usual response. "Mom—I'm taking my violin with me to Monica's—is that okay?"

"Oh, Sylvia told me you offered to lend Mr. Pratt your

131

instrument. That's so sweet. Is he going to take you up on it?"

"Maybe," Alan said. It wasn't a lie, exactly, but a convenient explanation anyway. For now.

*   *   *

Ziggy and Josée arrived in Vati's cab just before noon, and Vati came in with them. Ziggy's Vati was in his seventies —a big man with a mane of shaggy white hair.

"How's life treating you, Erich?" Mrs. Nearing said.

"Well enough, *danke,*" he said. "I just wanted to check with you that this place where Sigmund is spending all his time is…all right. You know—the people. They are good? They don't mind the intrusion?"

"Very good, very fine citizens," Mrs. Nearing said. "Pillars of the community, Erich, and they have a lovely daughter, Monica, who has made friends with our kids, and they all get along so well."

"*Gut.* Sigmund said so, but I thought I should make sure."

"They have kayaks, Vati," Ziggy said. "We should get one. You'd really like it."

Vati gave a booming laugh. "No, no, my boy. I'd get stuck like a pig in a bucket. You'd never get me out. No— I'll stick to my canoe, *vielen Dank.* If I ever get it back, that is."

"We're taking good care of it," Ziggy said. "Don't worry." If Ziggy's Vati knew where they had been in his canoe, against all the rules, he might be very worried indeed, Alan thought. Vati stayed for a cup of tea and then went on his way, telling Ziggy he would see him at the concert.

"Everybody's going," Mrs. Nearing said. Her cheeks were pink with excitement. "This is going to be a huge success for the Music Society. It's such a pity that Mr. Pratt won't be able to play his famous instrument, though. Oh—that reminds me—the police officer called this morning to say that they wouldn't need your fingerprints after all. I think perhaps they have a lead, or something. Anyway, I hope you're not too disappointed. Candace, of course, was delighted."

"I'll bet," Alan said. He exchanged looks with the others. Did that mean that Mr. Pratt had told on Dylan? They would find out soon enough, when they got to Monica's. If the police were there to arrest her brother, the whole overnight thing would be off, that was for sure. Alan felt guilty thinking like that, but he couldn't help it. His plan to get the Stradder back *included* Dylan, for one thing. And staying at Monica's was fun.

"We won't get the tour of the police headquarters after all?" Ziggy asked. "Crud. I wanted to see the lock-up where they keep the prisoners."

"They don't have a lock-up in Laingford," Josée said. "They take them to Port Francis. Mamère told me."

"She knows an awful lot for a prison cook," Ziggy said.

"That's where the best gossip always is—the kitchen," said Josée.

They piled into the Nearing van and, true to her word, Mrs. Nearing bought them all cones at the Treatstop on

133

the way. Josée asked for a little styrofoam cup of double chocolate to give to Monica.

"If we can sneak it past her mother," she said.

"Monica's not allergic, is she?" Mrs. Nearing said.

"No, her mom just watches everything Monica eats," Alan said. "She's a diet freak."

"That's not a very kind expression, Alan."

"Well, she is."

"I can't imagine why. That girl's too thin as it is."

"You might want to mention that to Mrs. Weems," Alan said.

"Perhaps I will. Poor girl."

*   *   *

The Weems's driveway was full of catering and florists' vans. Monica met them at the door.

"It's nuts in there," she said. "Mother's in high-party-mode, and the best thing to do is stay out of the way. Hi, Mrs. Nearing. Mother said to go on in. She wants your advice about the flower arrangements, she said."

"Thanks, dear. Now, you all be good tonight, okay? I'll be too busy to keep an eye on you, so I'm relying on you to be responsible."

"We don't need anyone keeping an eye on us, Mom," Alan said. Especially not in the next couple of hours, he added, in his mind. His mother disappeared in a flurry of people in uniforms, carrying trays.

"Can I put this in your room?" Josée asked Monica. She had something on a hanger, her clothes for the

134

concert. "I don't want to get it wrinkled. Mamère said it's a nightmare to iron. Oh, and here." She handed the cup of ice cream to Monica.

"Wow, thanks!" Monica said. "We only had salad for lunch. I'm starving."

"Is Dylan around?" Alan asked her.

"I don't know. Maybe," she said. "He was out on the jet ski earlier." She looked at the violin case in his hand. "Are you going to do it now?"

"The sooner the better, while everyody's busy here," Alan said.

"Okay—we'll meet you guys down at the boathouse in a few minutes," she said. "Come on, Josée. I want to show you what I'm wearing tonight."

Alan looked at Ziggy. "What are *you* wearing tonight?" he said. Ziggy looked glum and held up a small overnight bag. "Vati insisted," he said. "The works. Black pants. White shirt. Shoes."

"Me, too. I left mine in the van. Wait a sec." Alan went back to get the bag that his mother had handed to him before they left. He couldn't wait until he was old enough to be a professional detective. In all the books he'd read, they slouched around in trench coats and cool hats.

"Nobody makes a detective wear a white shirt and dress pants," he said to Ziggy as they went inside to put the bags in their guest room.

"What about James Bond?" Ziggy said. "He wears a tuxedo all the time."

"Yeah, but he gets to pick when," Alan said.

*   *   *

Down at the boathouse, they knew right away Dylan was there, because his music was making ripples in the water around the moored boats.

"How come your brother isn't deaf?" Josée asked Monica as they climbed the stairs.

"My dad says teenagers have Teflon eardrums," Monica said. "Whatever that means."

Dylan was lying on the sofa, reading a motorcycle magazine.

"What do *you* want?" he said as they gathered at the top of the stairs. "Get out of here."

Monica marched over and turned the music down. Dylan stood up, angry. "Hey—leave that alone," he said.

"We just want to talk to you," she said.

"Well, I don't want to talk to you, so bug off."

"Dylan," Alan said. "We know you didn't take the violin, okay? But Mr. Pratt thinks so, at least until this afternoon, he did."

Dylan's eyes narrowed.

"What happened this afternoon?" he said.

"Yes, what?" Monica said. Josée hadn't told her, then. Alan gave a brief account of the conversation he had overheard between Mr. Pratt and Annette. Dylan didn't interrupt, just stood there, listening. When Alan finished, he shrugged.

"So—the guy was loaded, anyone could tell that. But I didn't see him flaked out on the patio. I wasn't even there. It's his word against mine, and I didn't touch the stupid violin, okay?"

"But Dylan, don't you see?" Monica said. "If he saw you—I bet you were coming back from doing something illegal with those friends of yours—if he saw you, then he's going to tell the police, whether he thinks that lady violin player is involved or not. They're going to come and question you, at least. Dad'll go ballistic."

"I shoved a note under his door this morning—Mr. Pratt, I mean," Dylan said. "I told him I didn't have it." He was starting to look scared. His eyes were big, and his face was drained of colour.

"Do you think he believed you?" Alan said. "Look, if he doesn't get the violin back soon, he's going to go to the police. That's what he said."

"But I don't *have* it," Dylan said.

"We know that. But we know who does," Alan said. Dylan went very still.

"Who?"

"We need your help to get it back," Alan continued. "Then, when it magically reappears, nobody gets in trouble and everybody's happy. You're in the clear."

"Who has it?" he said.

"If I tell you, will you help?"

"Maybe. Who?"

"Eubie Sadler."

Dylan burst out laughing. "That old guy? You have to be joking. You want me to help you get something from him? That guy hates my guts, man. He tried to kill me."

Sixteen

He tried to *kill* you? When?" Monica almost screamed.

"I bet I know," Ziggy said. "Remember when we saw Mr. Sadler rowing down the river to town—when we were up at the lookout?" The others nodded. Ziggy turned to Dylan. "He tried to whack you with an oar, didn't he?"

"Damn right," Dylan said. "You saw that, huh? Bully for you. So you know he's a crazy man."

"How come, though?" Monica said. "Why would he attack you?"

"I was just trying to talk to him," Dylan said.

"At the crack of dawn," Alan added.

"So? I'm an early riser."

"What did you have to talk to him about?"

"Look, I don't need to answer the questions of a stupid bunch of little kids," he said. "Why don't you scram, okay? I'm not helping you. I'm sure not going over to that island, if that's what you're thinking."

"But you've been there before, haven't you?" Alan said. "You and your friends trashed the place, didn't you? And stole his violin and tossed it in the water."

138

"I wasn't involved. I stayed down with the boat…
Hey—how did you know about that?" Dylan asked.

"You just told me," Alan said. It was a classic detective-
move. Oddly, he didn't feel very good about it. Suddenly,
Dylan deflated like a pricked balloon and collapsed on
the sofa. There was a terrible silence.

"That was an awful thing to do, Dylan," Monica said
softly. "Those words…"

"What words?" Dylan said. He didn't seem all that
scary any more.

"Those words you wrote on his walls. How could you?"

"It wasn't me, Monica, I swear. I went with them, but
I didn't want to…oh, jeez."

"So what did you want to talk to him about, on the
river?" Alan persisted. A good detective was supposed to
stick to the point and not feel sorry for the witness.

"I went to apologize," Dylan said, looking at the floor.
"The others—they took his violin and smashed it against
the side of the boat. Then they threw it overboard. And
when we were leaving—we were in Spike's boat—that's
my friend—the old guy came back from wherever he had
been—fishing, maybe. He saw us and yelled at us. I
couldn't sleep all night. And the next day, I saw him
rowing into town, and I thought he was going to the
cops, so I went to try and, you know, apologize. I offered
him money. That's when he tried to kill me with his oar."

"But he didn't go to the cops," Alan said.

"No, I guess not."

"What about the oar? How did that end up in the
marsh?" Monica asked.

"I was mad, I guess. I went into town later and saw his boat and scoffed it—the oar, I mean."

"Smooth move," Ziggy said.

"I don't know, I was just trying to slow him down. Get back at him. Something. I thought he was about to ruin my life."

"Ruin *your* life?" Monica said. "You're the one who busted his violin and trashed his place."

"That wasn't me," Dylan said. "I just drove the getaway boat."

"You're pathetic," Monica said. She meant it. She walked over to the window and stood with her back to everybody, looking out over the lake. Alan thought she might be crying. There was a long silence.

"Dylan, we can fix this," he said.

"How?"

"I just need you to drive me over to the island, that's all. You can stay in the 'getaway boat'."

"What makes you think he's going to give *you* the violin? You're not the police. You're just a kid."

"This," Alan said, lifting his violin case. "I'm going to give him mine in exchange."

*   *   *

There wasn't time to canoe over to the island. They had decided that, already. But the jet ski would do it in no time. They had two hours before everybody was supposed to leave together for the concert. Ziggy and the girls promised to distract the grown-ups if need be, while

Dylan and Alan went to Sadler's Island.

"They know I can take ages getting ready," Monica said. "I'll pull that one if I have to. Dad will wait. I'm his little princess."

"Ew," said Josée.

"Sans blague," said Monica, with a grin. "But it comes in handy."

Alan got behind Dylan on the jet ski, the violin case sandwiched between them.

"You want to go fast?" Dylan said, once they were away from the dock.

"Why not?" Alan said, then wished he hadn't. Jet skis sure could boot it. They were across the bay in less than five minutes.

"You stay down here," Alan said when they got to Mr. Sadler's wharf. The last little bit they'd done slowly and quietly. There was no point in letting Mr. Sadler know Dylan was visiting. It was better if he didn't hear the sound of a jet ski. He would think it was trouble. He might even have a gun—you never knew.

This time, Alan stayed on the stairs leading up to the cabin. He went right up to the front door and knocked. No answer. But the rowboat was tied up down at the wharf, so the old man couldn't have gone anywhere. Unless he was walking around on the island somewhere. Alan knocked again, and listened. Very faintly, he heard something that sounded like "come in."

Eubie Sadler was lying on the couch in the living room, his face grey.

"I thought you were the police," he said.

"No, it's just me."

"You know, the police came for me once before, a long, long time ago. I hid in the closet."

"That was…?"

"The Holocaust. You'll have done it in school," he said.

"Yes, we did," Alan said. "You escaped?"

"Barely. Came to Canada for a new life. Those words, boy. Those words on my walls—it was like it was all happening again."

"Jeez, I'm sorry, Mr. Sadler. It must have been… awful."

"It was. What do you want?"

"I came to take the Stradivarius back. I haven't told anybody, but I know you have it."

"I do. How did you know?"

Alan explained how he and Josée had spied on him. How they had heard him playing it.

"I knew I couldn't keep it for ever," Eubie Sadler said. "After those punks came and took my Marta away—I called her that, you know—my violin—I was beside myself."

"I bet," Alan said.

"Then the next night, I heard music from that place over there, the place where that boy lives. Where that man lives who wants to take my island. Violin music. I thought somehow they had Marta, so late at night, I rowed over there."

"And you found a violin on the patio," Alan guessed.

"I was half out of my mind, maybe," Mr. Sadler said. "The music drew me like a moth to a flame. There was a boy there, a boy I'd never seen before, asleep on the ground. He looked like me—a much younger me. Maybe he was dead. I didn't know. But there was a violin. It was like a gift. I knew it wasn't Marta, but it was a violin. I didn't know until I got it home that it was…what it was. I knew it was only a matter of time before the police found me."

"The police don't know anything about it."

"But they are looking."

"Oh, yes. They're looking. Are you okay? You look kind of sick."

"Just my heart, boy. It's breaking, maybe."

"Mr. Sadler, nobody but us kids knows that you have the Stradder. I'm really sorry about your violin, and I know that one person who was involved in that break-in at your place is sorry, too."

"The Weems boy."

"Yes. He wasn't really here. At least, he stayed down at the boat."

"You know, young man, the people those many years ago, who watched when my people were herded onto cattle cars, they were like the boy who stayed down at the boat, too."

"I guess," Alan said. This wasn't going to work. He knew it. He could see the Stradder from where he was standing, by the door. The case was open on the floor, and Mr. Sadler's fingers caressed the priceless violin as he talked. "Can I get you anything?" he asked. "A glass of water? Your pills, maybe?"

"You're a good boy," Mr. Sadler said. "What's that you've got there?"

"It's...well. I though you might be willing to do a deal," he said.

"A deal?" Mr. Sadler laughed—a wheezy, painful sound. "You sound like Mr. Weems. He wants to turn my island into a condominium development," he said.

"But you won't let him," Alan said.

"Not while I'm still alive, at any rate. So what's your deal, young fellow?"

*   *   *

Alan cradled the Stradder carefully in his arms on the way back, and insisted that Dylan drive slowly, afraid that the splashing water might mark up the leather case. The others were waiting at the boathouse dock.

"Enfin! Did you get it?" Josée said, her voice high and tense.

"Oui, bien sûr," Alan said, trying out his clunky school French and grinning from ear to ear. "Now, how do we get it to the concert hall?"

"Oh—I told Mother you were bringing your own violin, in case Mr. Pratt needed it," Monica said. "She thought it was so cute. She won't even notice that it's a different case."

"Dylan, thanks, eh? You were great," Alan said. Dylan had stopped being a bully in Alan's mind. He was still a bit of a creep, perhaps, but you can't ride around on a jet ski with someone and still be afraid of them afterwards.

"No problem, dude," Dylan said, and slapped his hand. It was a good moment.

144

"Are you coming to the concert, Dylan?" Monica asked.

"I'm supposed to. Not that I'm a big fan of classical music, little sister. But I said I would go," he said. They all headed up to the house.

Not long afterwards, they were all ready to go. Mr. Pratt had already left in a limo that had come to pick him up, courtesy of Mr. Weems.

"Don't we all look marvellous?" Mrs. Weems said. "You'd never know this was Laingford." She was wearing a sea-green, glittery dress that reminded Alan of a mermaid movie he'd once seen. Mr. Weems looked like James Bond, and Dylan did, too.

"Wow," Josée whispered to Monica. "Your brother's hot." Alan had never heard her say anything like that before. He made a face at Ziggy, who made one back. Dylan did look a lot older than fifteen, though, all of a sudden. Monica and Josée were dressed up like Candace on a Leonardo DiCaprio day, and he thought they might be wearing makeup. Alan felt like a waiter, in his white shirt and shoes.

"No sweat," Ziggy whispered to him. "Maybe somebody will ask us to get them some wine."

Just as they were heading out the door, a police car pulled into the driveway. The flashers weren't going, but everybody froze, like deer caught in the headlights.

An officer got out of the cruiser and walked over to them. "Is Dylan Weems here?" she said.

Seventeen

Yes, he is," Mr. Weems said, putting his hand on Dylan's shoulder and stepping forward. "How can we help you, ma'am?" Alan noticed the surprised glance Dylan gave his father.

"Dylan, I'm Constable Mills, Ontario Provincial Police," she said. "We'd like to ask you some questions concerning a number of recent break-ins in the area. Is there somewhere private we can go?"

Mr. Weems nodded. Alan wondered what he was thinking. Was he really mad and trying not to show it, or was this what he looked like just before he blew up? Monica had told them what to expect, but she hadn't spelled it out.

"Sylvia," he said to Mrs. Weems. "You go on ahead with the kids. I'll stay with Dylan, and we'll join you at the auditorium later."

"Giles, are you sure…?" she said.

"Yes. Here—give this to Mary-Anne Nearing, would you? She's the vice president of the society, so she'll have to give the opening speech." He handed over a sheaf of notes from his jacket pocket. Great, Alan thought. Mom will freak.

"Thanks, Dad," Dylan said quietly. Then he looked up at Constable Mills. "Let's go and get this over with," he said. Before he turned back into the house, he caught Alan's eye. His face looked pretty scared, but Alan was sure he saw Dylan wink at him—just once, very quickly.

"You kids get in the car," Mrs. Weems ordered. "I'll be there in a minute."

"Did he just wink at you?" Ziggy asked, as they climbed in.

"I think he was telling me that he wasn't going to blab about the Stradder," Alan said. "At least I hope that's what he meant." They all stared for a moment at the brown leather case in Alan's lap.

"Put it under the seat," Monica said. "This is just awful." Mrs. Weems got into the driver's seat a moment later, her whole body announcing that everybody should keep quiet.

"Mother, what's going to happen to him?" Monica asked, anyway.

"I don't know, Monica, and I'd rather not talk about it," Mrs. Weems said. "His father's there to defend him if he needs it."

Nobody said another word, all the way to the concert hall.

Before they got out of the car, Mrs. Weems reached into her glittery little purse.

"Here are your tickets," she said, handing them out. "And here's some money for pop at the intermission. I don't want to see or hear you for the rest of the evening. Behave." Then she opened the door and marched towards the entrance like a general in an evening dress.

"Yikes," Ziggy said. "She's scary."

"She's furious. The timing couldn't have been worse," Monica said. "She'll be doing damage control for the rest of the night."

"It was nice of her to remember the tickets and everything," Josée said.

"Yeah, and she'll be too busy to think about us, which is perfect for what we have to do," Alan said. He pulled the violin case out from under the seat. "I think the best thing would be for me to go, and you others stand lookout," he said. "Then if there's trouble, you guys are out of it."

"If you meet anybody, you can just say you're going to get Mr. Pratt's autograph," Josée said.

"At least there's hardly anybody here yet," Monica said. "We're really early."

"Yeah, look, the orchestra members are only just arriving," Ziggy said. The musicians, in groups of two and three, were entering the building, carrying instrument cases.

"Should we wrap it up before we take it in?" Monica asked. "There's a blanket in the back."

"No," Ziggy said. "People would notice a covered-up object. But look, practically everybody's carrying an instrument case. Alan will just blend in."

"Okay, then—let's go."

Ziggy was right. There was a crowd at the door, and they just went with it. Nobody was taking tickets yet, even. The musicians headed for the dressing room area and Alan joined them, like a small fish swimming with

148

bigger ones. Nobody gave him a second glance.

Ziggy, Josée and Monica followed as far as the end of the dressing room hallway and leaned up against the walls out of the way, like they were just waiting for the concert to get going.

"We're supposed to be bored, don't forget," Monica whispered. "That's what people will expect." Immediately, they each assumed that blank expression that says "I'd rather be at home watching TV."

Alan knew the next bit was going to be tricky. If Mr. Pratt was already in his dressing room, Alan would have to hide until he came out. The plan was to leave the Stradder there anonymously. He had remembered to bring a cloth to wipe the case clean of fingerprints—he just hoped he would have time to do it. He would have worn gloves, but it would have looked funny. Just then, an announcement came over the intercom in the hallway.

"Attention please, ladies and gentlemen. This is your one-hour call. One hour to curtain. Please come onstage now for a sound and light check." Moments later, the dressing room doors opened, and the hall was full of people. Alan stood flat against the wall, and nobody seemed to notice him. Even Mr. Pratt himself pushed past him unseeing and joined the crowd moving into the auditorium. Alan remembered how he himself usually felt before one of Mr. Ziegler's recitals. He recognized the distracted expression on Mr. Pratt's face. He'd seen it himself in his own mirror. Wow, he thought. Even virtuosos get nervous before performing.

This was the perfect opportunity, and probably the only

chance he was going to get. Once the hallway was clear, he slipped quickly into Mr. Pratt's dressing room, put the Stradder down on the dressing table, gave it a fast wipe with the cloth in his pocket and slipped out again. The hall was still empty, and Alan tried to saunter casually back out to the lobby, even though he felt like running as fast as he could. His heart was pounding so hard, he could hear it.

"Succès?" Josée said. Alan nodded.

"I think we should go into the auditorium and find our seats," Monica said. "If we stay there until the concert starts, we'll have an alibi."

"Good plan," Alan said, and they did.

The next hour was busy. The orchestra tuned up, and then the lighting people rehearsed the spotlight that was supposed to follow the conductor and Mr. Pratt. One of the orchestra members complained that his music stand light was burnt out, and somebody fixed it. Then there was an argument about the microphones. Through it all, the orchestra members talked and moved around. Some left and came back again. Latecomers arrived and took their places onstage. Mr. Pratt waited patiently in a chair beside the curtain.

"Why doesn't he have a hissy fit and go to his dressing room?" Ziggy said in frustration. "The suspense is killing me."

"Me, too," Alan admitted. "Still, the later he finds it, the better. More suspects that way. Less chance anybody'll think of us."

"When he does find it, I bet they'll call the police," Josée said. "There'll be a big fuss."

"Yeah, they may not even let him play it," Ziggy said.

"They'll want to take it away for fingerprints."

"It's okay. I wiped it," Alan said.

Finally, half an hour before the concert was supposed to start, the stage was cleared, and everybody went backstage. The doors to the auditorium opened, and the audience poured in. Fifteen minutes later, everything was still calm. Alan was watching the hallway carefully. There were a couple of openings into the auditorium from the hall, and you could see whoever was passing by. He was watching for a sudden bustle, maybe some blue uniforms. Nothing.

"He can't have missed it, can he?" Monica whispered. They were surrounded by others at this point, hemmed in my adults on either side. Their seats were near the front, and if anyone got up at this point, four hundred people would see them.

"Where did you leave it?" Ziggy asked Alan.

"Right there on the counter, next to his hairbrush," Alan said. "It would be in his face as soon as he walked in."

"Then he must have decided to keep it quiet," Josée said.

"I guess he wants to play it first," Alan said.

The lights in the auditorium dimmed a bit, and the orchestra began filing onstage. There was a smattering of applause while they settled, then the lights went out completely and the evening began.

Mrs. Nearing did a fine job of the welcoming speech, Alan thought. He was nervous for her sake, but she seemed perfectly natural and relaxed up there. He knew how much she hated public speaking and clapped extra loud when she was finished.

"That was short," Monica said, leaning over Ziggy and Josée to get Alan's attention. "My dad would still be talking." They grinned at each other.

In her speech, Mrs. Nearing had not mentioned the Stradder at all. She just talked about how wonderful Mr. Pratt was and how lucky the town was to get him for a concert. Not long after that, he made his entrance.

Something magical seemed to happen to Mr. Pratt when he was in front of an audience, Alan thought. He got bigger, somehow, more real. You couldn't stop looking at him.

"It must be weird to be that magnetic," he whispered to Ziggy.

"I think it would be tiring," Ziggy whispered back.

Then Mr. Pratt lifted his violin, tucked it under his chin and began to play. It was the Stradder, no question. Its mellow voice reached out over the audience like a wave of warm, scented air, and everybody sat up a little straighter in their chairs. Alan felt goosebumps begin on his arms.

When Mr. Pratt had played on the lakeside patio, it had seemed like a beam of light, rippling out over the water. This time, backed with a full orchestra inside a concert hall, it was more like a bonfire.

At the intermission, they filed out with the rest of the audience and stood in line to buy refreshments. Everybody was chattering, though Alan could tell that not everybody was talking about the Stradder, or even about the music. Most of the people probably didn't even know the violin had been stolen in the first place. It made him feel a little less nervous. Surely, there must be some sort of reaction from somebody, now that it was obvious that Mr. Pratt had his violin back.

He caught a glimpse of Candace, talking excitedly to a group of her friends. She was probably telling them that she and Mr. Pratt were old buddies. He wondered if Mr. Pratt had ended up hurting her feelings as he'd done to Monica. Never mind, he told himself. Even if her encounter with the famous musician wasn't perfect, he would bet that she would still brag about it for years.

They took their cans of pop to the wall outside the backstage entrance, and leaned against it again. Mrs. Nearing came out with Mrs. Weems, both deep in conversation. Mrs. Nearing noticed them first.

"Enjoying the concert?" she said.

"It's amazing," Alan said. "To be able to play like that."

"What's also amazing is that the Stradivarius has been returned," she said. "You wouldn't know anything about that, would you?" She was looking very carefully at each of them.

"That's *fantastique,* Madame Nearing," Josée said, her eyes wide and innocent.

"Yeah, wow!" said Ziggy.

"Do they know who returned it?" Monica asked.

"Mr. Pratt must be really happy," Alan said.

"Mr. Pratt is not opening his door to visitors until after the concert," Mrs. Weems said, her lips tight. "But I should imagine he's delighted." She turned her ice-blue gaze on Mrs. Nearing. "We'll inform the police after this is over, and not before, I think, Mary-Anne," she said. It was not a question. "I'll go and speak to the management. We don't want them barging in and ruining a perfectly lovely evening—any more than they have done already," she added. Off they went, Mrs. Nearing giving them a backward glance that meant there would be more questions later.

"Hey, look, Monica. Your brother," Josée said. "He's not in jail after all." Dylan was making his way through the crowd towards them.

"Dylan!" Monica said, and sort of hugged him, which made his face go red. "You're free!"

"Not exactly," Dylan said. "I'm going to be charged, but Dad talked them out of locking me up. He was great. He was really mad, but great."

"What happened? Did they ask about the violin?" Alan said.

"Nope, just the break-in stuff. Spike and Gord, the guys that were with me yesterday, got caught red-handed today, and they named me as one of their gang. I'm not, really. I just hid some of their stuff. I told them that, and I think it's going to be okay."

"But you're still being charged?"

"Receiving stolen goods," Dylan said. He sounded kind of proud of it, but Alan knew better than to say so.

"Will you go to jail?" Monica said.

"I don't think so. Dad thinks probation, probably. And he's sending me to that school, for sure, now."

"What school?" Ziggy said. "How come Monica goes to a private school, and you go to high school here?"

"He keeps getting kicked out of the private ones," Monica said.

"Yeah, but this place is different. It's a military college," Dylan said.

"You *want* to go there?" she said. "Why didn't you say so before?"

"Nobody asked me," he said, and grinned. "I gotta go and sit with Dad. I'm like chained to him from now on." He didn't seem too unhappy about it, either, Alan thought. Dylan turned to look at him. "Mr. Pratt got the violin back okay?"

"I left it in his dressing room—nobody saw me. He's been playing it," Alan said. "But we don't think he can have talked to anybody about it, yet. Not until after the concert, anyway."

"Well, I just wanted to let you know that I didn't squeal on you, dude."

"Thanks…dude," Alan said.

*   *   *

After the concert, after the dozen or so curtain calls and the standing ovation for Mr. Pratt, the lights came up, and people began to leave. Mrs. Weems hurried over to collect them.

"We have to rush back before everybody gets there for the reception," she said. She'd cheered up a bit, Alan thought, and her eyes were sparkling.

"Did they call the police about the violin?" Monica asked her.

"I wouldn't know. If Mr. Pratt chooses to believe that it was a joke all along, that's his business," she said. "It's what he just told me, anyway. Come on."

Epilogue

The moon was full over Steamboat Lake. At a point of land at the end of the bay, a party was going on—a good party, by the sound of it. There was laughter and music and the tinkling of glasses. If you went closer, you'd catch the scent of grilled meat and pine-scented earth, night-blooming flowers and expensive perfume.

Near the shore, a canoe moved silently through the mirror-still water. There were four figures in the boat, two of them paddling, the other two trailing their fingers through the water as the boat glided among the reeds.

"Way to get permission from your mom," Ziggy said, steering lazily around a log sticking up out of the water. "Asking her while she's in the middle of a conversation with the mayor. Good move."

"She said yes, though, didn't she? As long as we didn't go too far," Alan said.

"Maybe she'd let us go on a canoe trip before we go back to school," Josée said.

"Hardly," Ziggy said. "Not when she finds out what really happened. Alan will have to tell her some of it, eventually, then he'll be grounded for the rest of his life."

"That's true," Josée said. "I guess she'll notice at some point that your violin has disappeared, eh, Alain?"

"You don't think she'll believe me when I tell her I lost it?" Alan said, turning around to grin at her. They were far enough away from the party that they couldn't hear it any more. Instead, another kind of music came softly and sweetly over the water from Sadler's Island. It was an old-fashioned dance tune, played on a violin.

"Yep. Grounded forever," Ziggy said.

"Probably. But it was worth it," Alan said.

Chapter One of
The Pioneer Poltergeist
Alan Nearing Mystery #2
Coming in 2007!

"How can two goats and a donkey produce so much…manure?" Alan wanted to use a stronger word for the stuff, but was saving it for when he was mad enough. He blew out a breath to get a flop of hair out of his eyes and took a better grip on his shovel.

"It's just grass and mulched veggies," Ziggy said. "Think of it as backyard compost."

"Still stinks."

It was their first day on the job as go-fers at Laingford Pioneer Village Park.

"Go-fer means you're the one who goes-fer things," Alan's mother had explained. "Kind of a messenger and helper on the site. And you'll be wearing pioneer costumes, like in a play. It'll be fun."

It had sounded like a good idea at the time. They were going to be paid for the work, even though they were only twelve, and anything had to be better than mowing lawns, which is what they usually did to earn back-to-school money. So, Alan and his friends Ziggy and Josée were spending the last two weeks of August working at the Park, before school started.

Their job, as explained when they had arrived that morning, was simple. "Just make yourselves useful," the staff supervisor had said. She looked like someone's saintly old grandma, in a long dress and shawl, but she obviously ruled the place. "All the staff have jobs to do around here," she had said, "and they'll be glad of the help. They'll send you back and forth with messages, too. We don't use walkie-talkies here, except when there's trouble. They ruin the atmosphere."

Alan and Ziggy had been given overalls, boots and straw hats. Josée was handed a long skirt and a sunbonnet.

Now, Alan was working himself up into a temper. "I thought we would be doing things like chopping wood and carrying axes around," he said. "Maybe grabbing a nap under a tree."

Josée got to sit in a shady courtyard, helping a lady make candles. Alan and Ziggy, however, were asked to muck out the animal pens with wooden-handled shovels, the old-fashioned way, to show the tourists how it used to be done. In the evening, when the Park was closed, the maintenance guy, Sheldon, would clear out the pens properly with a miniature backhoe, but the boys were to do as much as they could by hand, for show. And they weren't allowed to go near the backhoe.

"This is my baby," Sheldon had said when he was showing them around the maintenance hut.

"I can see that," Alan had said, and Ziggy had poked him. The machine was hidden under a blanket, like a horse. It was orange and chrome, gleaming with polish and oil, and Sheldon was patting the side of it. He kept the keys on a chain attached to his pants, so they knew he was serious about the No Touch rule. Alan figured they wouldn't be getting backhoe-driving lessons any time soon.

Instead, they were shovelling poo.

"Think of the money, Alan," Ziggy said as they worked. "Your mother promised that you wouldn't have to put it into your college fund, right? You can spend it on anything you want."

"If this is the kind of work we have to do for two weeks, I'll be spending it all on deodorant," Alan said, wishing that Josée was there with them, shovelling too. She'd be agreeing with him and cracking jokes, not trying to make him like it.

The animal pen and its manure pile was next to a log cabin, part of an old-fashioned homestead, one of many on the property. Along with the houses, the pioneer village included an inn, a blacksmith shop, a general store, church, school and meeting house, all filled with staff and volunteers in costume, doing the kind of things people used to do back in the 1800s. The log cabin, (called the Fergusson House on the village map) was where Josée was working. There was an open fire pit in the courtyard, with a big kettle of wax suspended over it. A woman used a ladle to fill long, thin cans with the hot wax, which she brought over to the table where Josée and several visitors were standing. You took a piece of string and dipped it, over and over, into the wax, and slowly, it became a candle. It looked like Josée was enjoying herself, chatting with the tourists and laughing. As the boys looked over at her, she looked up and gave them a wave. Then she said something to a couple of kids who were part of the tourist group, and they headed over to the boys.

"This is where we're supposed to pretend to be pioneers," Ziggy said. "What do we say?"

Alan, who had acted in a couple of school plays, said "Leave it to me."

The kids, a boy and girl of about seven, approached and leaned over the fence that separated them.

"Aren't you afraid of the animals?" the girl said. "Do they bite?"

Fred the donkey was standing a few feet away, munching a mouthful of grass and gazing off into the distance. The two goats, Gertie and Alice, were lying in the shade, still as shadows. It was hot, the sun was blazing down, and nobody was moving who didn't have to.

"Nah, they're totally tame," Alan said. "Back in the old days, kids would ride the donkey to school, even."

"Do you ride him?" the boy asked.

"I could, but we've got work to do here."

"Isn't that really gross, what you're doing?"

"You get used to it," Ziggy said. "People had to work a lot harder back then. They made you get up at, like, four a.m. and go and feed the chickens and milk the cows or goats or whatever and then you had to walk ten kilometres to school in blizzards and sit in a freezing room with no internet."

"Ew," the girl said. "But you'd get to ride the donkey to school in the blizzard, right?"

"Not in the winter. Donkeys hibernate," Alan said.

"They do not," the boy said.

"This one does. He goes to a farm out in the country and sleeps in a barn all winter."

"So, do you guys live here all the time? Do you sleep in that little house?"

"No, we live in town," Alan said. "This is just a job, really." Both boys began shovelling again, to show the watching children what real old-fashioned work was like. Alan was beginning to feel a bit like something in a zoo, and he was hoping they would get bored and wander off, maybe go make some more candles over there in the shade.

Alan plunged the shovel down into the muck and there was a weird clang as he struck something hard. A horseshoe, maybe? Or a donkey shoe? He used the tip of the shovel to scrape the dirty straw away, and then gasped. Ziggy, looking down too, whispered, "Holy cow." Before the children could see what he had uncovered, Alan quickly booted a bit of straw over it.

"Hey kids," he said, turning back to them. "We have to do some work now, or we'll get into trouble. You'd better go back to your parents." Both children looked surprised and hurt for a moment, then the boy shrugged.

"When I grow up, I'm going to be a computer scientist," he said. "I won't have to take a dumb, stinky job like you have, anyway. C'mon, Lisa." They turned their backs on the boys and returned to the candle-making area.

"That was smooth," Ziggy said, but they were both too excited to care much.

He flipped the covering straw back, and they both stared at what was there. Unmistakable, which is why

162

Alan had covered it up so quickly. Lying under the dirty straw they'd been shovelling was a very big, very dangerous-looking...

Photo by Carol McVittie

Mel Malton was born in England and emigrated with her family to Canada. She grew up in Bracebridge, Ontario and has resettled in the same area. After studying at the Ontario College of Art, she moved on to theatre studies at Ryerson Polytechnic University, followed by a year or two of English at Acadia University in Nova Scotia. Mel spent the next ten years touring North America in the professional theatre business as both actor and stage manager.

Mel's crime stories have appeared in many anthologies. Her first mystery novel for adults, *Down in the Dumps*, was short-listed for an Arthur Ellis Award for Best First Crime Novel. Her other adult mysteries are *Cue the Dead Guy, Dead Cow in Aisle Three* and *One Large Coffin To Go*.

Mel currently lives in a log cabin in Huntsville, Ontario, with her two dogs, Karma and Ego.